Mission: Saving Shayna
SEAL Team Phantom Book 5

By Elle Boon
elleboon@yahoo.com

D1559665

Mission Saving Shayna
SEAL Team Phantom Book 5
Copyright © 2016 Elle Boon
First E-book Publication: November 2016
Second E-book Publication: August 2018
Cover design by Valerie Tibbs of Tibbs Design
Edited by Tracy Roelle

Dedication

I'd like to thank Desiree Holt for always believing in me—without her, I wouldn't be where I am today as an author. This book was originally in her Omega Team world, but since that platform shutdown, I've done a little editing and changed a few character names. Other than that, the story is the same. From the bottom of my heart, I owe Ms. Holt so very much, it would take the rest of this book to show her the praise she is deserved. I hope everyone who reads Shayna and Mike's story fall in love with them the same as I did.

As always, thank you to my betas, my readers, and my family. Love y'all so hard.

Love,
Elle

Other Books by Elle Boon

Ravens of War
Selena's Men
Two For Tamara
Jaklyn's Saviors
Kira's Warriors

Mystic Wolves
Accidentally Wolf & His Perfect Wolf (1 Volume)
Jett's Wild Wolf
Bronx's Wounded Wolf
A Fey's Wolf

SmokeJumpers
FireStarter
Berserker's Rage
A SmokeJumpers Christmas
Mind Bender, Coming Soon

Iron Wolves MC
Lyric's Accidental Mate
Xan's Feisty Mate
Kellen's Tempting Mate
Slater's Enchanted Mate
Dark Lovers
Bodhi's Synful Mate
Turo's Fated Mate
Arynn's Chosen Mate
Coti's Unclaimed Mate

Miami Nights
Miami Inferno

Rescuing Miami

Standalone
Wild and Dirty

SEAL Team Phantom Series
Delta Salvation
Delta Recon
Delta Rogue

Delta Redemption
Mission Saving Shayna
Protecting Teagan

The Dark Legacy Series
Dark Embrace

Chapter One

Shayna tucked a strand of hair behind her ear, looking around the crowded airport nervously, her Guarius violin clenched in one hand while sweat trickled down her back. Having a thirty thousand dollar musical instrument hadn't seemed a big deal a couple weeks ago, but that was before she'd had a two million dollar Stradivarius violin stolen. Luckily the J&A Beare benefactor hadn't blamed her for the theft, and the precious violin had been insured. Still, knowing someone had been in her apartment while she'd been sleeping was creepy as hell. Not to mention she'd been getting threatening letters, and they'd been escalating. Enough so she finally came to the conclusion she needed to come home and seek a little help from her cousin Amelia.

Damn, Tampa was hotter than Hades in July. She pulled her hair back into a hairband, and looked for the nearest Starbucks. The picture of the liquid gold supplier was the first thing that had a smile forming on her lips. After ordering her vanilla latte with a double shot of espresso and one Sweet'N Low, she made her way out toward the baggage claim. She drank the entire thing by the time she made it to where her one piece of luggage would be coming out.

Tingles raced up her spine. A feeling of being watched had her looking behind her, but the busy terminal was too full for her to find anything out of the ordinary. "Just get your bag, and get out," she mumbled to herself. The view of all the luggage already starting to come out of the shoot was a welcome sight as she waited for the bright floral hard-shell case to appear.

The sound of a child's cry made her look up in time to see a little boy of about three racing toward her, his mother chasing him with an infant in a stroller. A pang of envy hit her at the image of the cute little guy, until he got closer and she could see his mother was losing him in the crowd. Without thinking twice, she moved into his trajectory, halting his escape. "Hey there, little man. Where are you off to?" Bright blue eyes blinked up at her out of a tear stained face. Keeping a firm hold on her violin case, she ruffled his hair. "My, you sure are a fast runner. I bet you ran like the wind. Yes, you did."

"Oh my god, thank you so much." The child's mother reached them, her face red from her exertion. "Alexander James. What have I told you about staying right beside mommy?" She grabbed him up into her arms, and snuggled her face into his neck.

Shayna stood up, looking down at the sleeping baby in the pink onesie. "I figured you needed a little help. He's a sprinter." Her hand ruffled the boy's hair.

"That he is. My husband is supposed to be meeting us." The blonde woman looked around, then eyes that were similar to her son's lit up. "Alex," she breathed.

Again, that pang of envy hit as the woman and her family went off to embrace the man who was clearly the husband and father. Looking back at the conveyer belt, the colorful bag sat along with several others making its way around the circular contraption. She'd been on tour for the last four months and had sent most of her things back to New York, where her apartment was. However, the large suitcase was packed to the seams with clothes and necessities. Things she figured she'd need while she was in Tampa figuring out who the hell was trying to ruin her career, and possibly kill her.

Reaching for her bag, she was nearly knocked over as the man next to her tried to grab his own. "Excuse me," she said looking up into a pair of wraparound shades. She'd shifted the violin case into her other hand, a fact she was grateful for since the man would have knocked into it as he jerked the banged up luggage off the platform and stomped away.

She had to wait for her own luggage to come around again, but then it was one of only a few pieces left, making it easy to grab and go. As she went to exit the airport, the couple and their two children waved at her. Not everyone was bad, but she couldn't shake the feeling of being watched.

Not wanting to alert anyone when she'd arrived, Shayna grabbed the first cab, allowing him to stow her large suitcase in the back. "I keep this with me." She patted her beloved violin.

"Whatever floats your boat. Where to?" The cab driver stared at her through the rearview mirror, waiting for directions.

The thought of going to a hotel first appealed only marginally. Instead, she gave him the address to the Alpha Team headquarters, then sat back with a sigh. For crying out loud, did the man not have air conditioning? She looked at his dash, and sure enough, he didn't have it on. Her eyes narrowed, having driven in cabs for the last few years all over New York City, she knew the way they worked. "Can you turn the air on please?" Her voice she kept low and sweet.

"Sorry, it's broken. You can roll a window down." He motioned toward the door.

With a nod, Shayna smiled. "Of course I can. I can also make sure my tip reflects my discomfort."

Looking at her skinny jeans tucked into the little suede calf boots and the plaid shirt over the tank, she probably looked like she was a tourist who had no clue. What he didn't notice was the bottom of the shoes were red, and they were not knockoffs, nor the fact the jeans and shirt probably cost more than his entire wardrobe. She looked at him as he drove through the crowded streets of Tampa, then grabbed her phone, figuring she should let Amelia know she was on her way. Her cousin's phone rang several times and just when she was sure it would go to voicemail, the woman answered, sounding out of breath.

"Shayna Macintyre, you best be calling to tell me when your flight gets in." Amelia's tone held an edge to it.

Biting her lip, she was glad her older cousin couldn't see the guilt. "Well, I sort of caught an earlier flight, and didn't want to bother you or Greg."

A spate of curse words filled the line, ones that Shayna had heard their mothers use on more than one occasion. "Now, that is just not nice. Not nice at all, Amelia Mejia. You kiss your mama with that mouth?"

"Oh, don't even go there with me. How long before you get here?"

She looked at the arrival time on the dash of the cab, then let Amelia know. "I'll see you in a few, and try to calm your temper by the time I get there. Maybe go and work it out with," Shayna paused and coughed before continuing. "You know, like a little bowchicawowow, or afternoon delight."

Amelia laughed. "We keep things strictly professional during office hours."

"How boring." Shayna loved to tease Amelia, especially since she was the one everyone called a total snooze fest.

"When you get here, I'll be sure and show you how boring I am, chica." Amelia's words held no heat.

Her palms were sweating, along with every other part of her body, by the time they entered the parking lot of the warehouse. From the outside it probably didn't look like much, but inside she knew it held the electronics to find out just about any information a person needed. Following the driver out of the cab, she kept a firm hand on her case while he hefted the colorful one out of the back. His glare at her and the surroundings, let her know he thought she was either crazy, or possibly going inside to record porn. She snorted at the last thought.

He named a figure for the fare, much higher than what she'd seen on the meter. "Good try, but not today, Satan. Not today." Already having pulled out the amount owed and added an extra five, which was five more than he deserved, she walked away without another word.

At the entrance she pushed the button to announce her arrival and waited. Since it was the weekend, the lot was pretty much empty except for a couple of vehicles. She looked over each one, figuring her cousin probably drove with Greg since they lived together, and the sharp little convertible probably belonged to one of their operatives. It amazed her to no end that she actually knew real life 007 types.

"Now, what has put that little grin on your face?" Amelia stood with a smirk on her gorgeous face. At thirty-four years old, she could pass for Shayna's sister, with her black hair and curvy figure. The only differences were Amelia had black as night eyes and hair, while Shayna had green ones rimmed with black and her hair was a dark red.

"I was just thinking you'd make an excellent Sean Connery." She kept her face straight as Amelia looked her up and down.

"Nah, I would look awful in a speedo. Come here, you."

****

Mike Royce watched Amelia pull the younger woman in for a hug, his lungs seizing in his chest. Shit! How the hell was he supposed to become a bodyguard, and try to figure out who the hell was trying to frame her for the theft of a two million dollar violin, if his dick was already standing at attention?

"You got that look you know?" Greg noted from beside him.

He blinked his eyes. "What look?"

Greg tilted his head toward the front of the building. "The one that says you just got kicked in the gut. Believe me, I know the look. Let me warn you now, that girl is family."

"I'm here to do a job. Pretty sure as soon as it's over, she's out of here, right?" Mike stood straight, towering over the older man. He'd been in the CIA for the last decade, taking early retirement. He'd recently relocated to Texas after his last mission, when his partner Maddox Lopez fell for a member of the Navy he was sent to investigate. Their two year undercover operation had worn on his nerves, but seeing his best friend and partner find the woman of his dreams, and nearly die, had made him rethink his own life. He wanted something that didn't have him being a different person for months, years at a time. Roots, that was what he'd craved. He and Maddox had both been on the same page, wanting to open their own personal security agency. When Greg had called, it had been a stroke of luck, or so he'd thought since Maddox was off with Hailey for a few weeks, leaving him with some spare time. Mike definitely didn't need the money since he was from what they called 'old money'. Luckily, he still had his family home in Tampa, which would play right into the assignment.

Greg put his hand on Mike's shoulder. "Just wanted you to understand what would happen should Amelia think you hurt her baby cousin. Trust me, this lecture is better coming from me."

His first instinct was to shrug off the other man's touch, but he realized Greg was only doing what Mike would do if he'd had a family who mattered. "I got it. Now, how about we get with the point of the meeting." Steel entered his voice, and veins.

Greg looked him up and down, then nodded. They went back into the breakroom, the area Amelia decided would be the best place to handle the situation. Hell, he didn't give two shits where it was handled, he just wanted to get the facts and move forward. That was his way of getting shit done.

Amelia and the angel…he wiped that train of thought away, turned his back so he didn't watch them make their way toward him and Greg. He went to the coffee station in the room where they were meeting, glad they hadn't skimped on the coffee or the maker. The scent of the fresh roast hit him immediately, making his fingers itch for the cup to fill. He lifted the styrofoam to his lips and took a fortifying sip before he turned, nearly colliding with the alluring woman. Damn!

"Excuse me. Can I get a cup of that?" Her eyes closed as she inhaled, making her chest lift.

Yeah, he was screwed, his eyes went straight to the white tank peeking out of the open shirt and couldn't miss the fact she had more than a handful. "Help yourself," he said gruffly, sidestepping away from her and the coffeemaker.

"Thank you. I have only a couple vices, and one of them is coffee. I don't want it, I need it. There's a difference you know."

He was not going to turn back around, Mike swore, but the humor in her husky voice had him doing that very thing. Big mistake. Huge. He'd gotten an eyeful of her front, and it was an exceptional view, but the back was just as wonderful, if not better. A high, rounded ass encased in a pair of jeans that looked like they were painted on. Fashion called them stretch denim, he called them perpetual hard-on makers. Of course, it depended on the woman wearing them, and this one wore them well.

"Ah, delicious," she sighed.

His mind went straight to the gutter as he thought of other things she'd say the same thing about. "Yeah, I like coffee, too." Mike nearly groaned out loud at the inane words, but then his eyes fell on the violin case she had yet to put down. "You want me to put that down for you?"

Her eyes widened, then she stepped back as if he'd just asked her to get naked and do the hokey pokey or some shit. "Um, no. I'm fine."

He shrugged then walked to where Greg and Amelia were going over notes on a laptop. Sitting across from them, he studied their body language, knowing they were as aware of him as he was of them.

"Mike Royce, this is Shayna Macintyre, my cousin. Shayna, this is Mike." Amelia finally looked up from the computer screen.

Sitting around the square table he tilted his head. "My friends call me Royce."

"My friends call me Shayna, but my family calls me Shayne. I will throat punch you if you call me Shayne." Sweetness dripped off her tongue.

"Why do they call you that then?" He had no clue why he'd asked, but the need to know more about her plagued him.

"Because my dad wanted a boy, and they were sure I was one. All through my mom's pregnancy he called her bump Shayne Junior, after him. When I came out a squalling girl, my mother added the a at the end. He still treated me like his son, until I decided I wanted to play the violin at the age of six instead of play ball. You'd think I committed a mortal sin," she laughed.

"I promise not to mistake you for a boy, or call you Shayne." He held up his hand. It was a promise he could make and keep.

"Speaking of violins. The Stradivarius hasn't been returned to the Beare foundation as of yet." Greg tapped his fingers on the table.

Shayna sucked in a breath. "I didn't think it would be. Whoever took it is probably aware of its age and value. I just wish they hadn't taken it from me, but at least they'd waited until the final concert was over."

Mike held up his hand. "Alright, let's pretend you are speaking to a third grader, and tell me what is so special about this particular violin."

The woman who entranced him with every move she made, narrowed green eyes on him. "The Stradivarius is a violin that was created in 1711. The sound is incomparable, although my Guarius is close. Nothing can quite compare with the unique superiorities the Stradivarius can create, especially when playing Bach. However, some say they can't tell the difference when they listen to the same played on a violin made in 2002 by Stefan-Peter Greiner, but I can. The big Romantic and 20th century concertos sound so much better on my baby, but even better on a Stradivarius." Passion made her face flush.

Royce wondered if she would look like that while making love, then stopped as he realized he had no clue what the hell she was talking about, nor did he think violins were the least bit sexy. "Alright, so this instrument is extremely expensive. How easy is it to offload it to a buyer?"

"That's just it. It is extremely difficult, if not close to impossible," Shayna said looking from one to the other until her eyes landed on Royce.

Chapter Two

Mike watched the flare of something undefinable wash over Shayna. "Explain," he instructed.

"There are not very many authentic Stradivarius violins in the world. The one I had on loan was actually one of the cheaper ones. I mean, one sold for like forty-eight million dollars. If my memory serves me correctly, there might be two that have been stolen in all of history, and never recovered because they are hard to sell off." She chewed on her bottom lip.

"Then what would this person get out of stealing the violin from you?" Royce looked to Greg and Amelia, wondering if they'd come up with a theory.

Greg raised his brow. "Maybe the thief was hired by a collector and this person wants it for his very own."

It was a possibility and one they couldn't discount. However that didn't explain the calls, or they could be a completely different threat. "These phone calls," he paused spearing Shayna with his stare. "Have they left a voicemail, anything we can trace?"

She shook her head, red hair glinting in the overhead light. "I've missed several unknown calls, and when I do answer, some have been heavy breathing, which is so cheesy." She took a breath. "But the one that sent me running here was truly scary."

He watched her body language as that was one of his specialties. Reading people. He'd been in the CIA long enough to tell when someone was lying, telling a partial truth, or was truly in fear. Shayna Macintyre radiated a deep seated terror. "Go on. Anything you say here will not be held against you." The fact he'd just said a line from part of the Miranda Rights had a grin kicking up the corner of his lips.

"I'm assuming it was a he, but it could very well have been a she because it was a computer like voice. They said, *you have one week to present*

yourself to me of your own freewill, or I'll take you.
If you make me do the latter, you won't like it, but I
will," she whispered as she finished.

Mike tapped his knuckles on the table. "Sounds to me like whoever took the violin may indeed be a collector, not just of violins, but of musicians as well. Have you checked to see if other women have gone missing who've played music similar to Miss. Macintyre?"

Amelia slapped her forehead. "Why didn't I think of that?" Then she snorted. "What do you think we are, amateurs?"

Although he knew the two members who'd started the Alpha Team were also a couple, they kept a strict policy of keeping their relationship professional as much as possible during office hours. However, sometimes, like now, Greg reached for the woman he loved. Mike looked down at the reports he'd been given, offering the couple a moment of privacy. When he looked back up, his gaze landed on the stunning green of Shayna.

"You must be incredibly talented if a collector wants you and your instrument." He nodded at the case she had yet to release. "Maybe we should put that in a safe here at the office until we find out who's responsible," he stated. The thought of not only guarding her, but the expensive musical instrument she didn't seem in any hurry to let go of wasn't too appealing. Scratch that. Guarding her was too damn appealing. The violin he could do without.

She shook her head, making the ponytail slap around. His mind envisioned grabbing the thick strands in his fist while he tilted her head back…before he could go any further with the fantasy, he pulled his head back to the job at hand. Saving Shayna was what he was hired to do, not getting into her pants.

"I already emailed Pam, she's our resident computer guru. If she can't find out if another brilliant musician such as yourself has gone missing, then there isn't one to be found." Amelia sat back with a frown.

Mike had only been around the woman a couple weeks, but he had learned to read her. "What's bothering you?"

Amelia reached across the table grabbing Shayna's hand. "You're going to need twenty-four hour protection, sweetie. I know you planned to hole up in a hotel, but that's not good enough. You're coming home with Greg and me," she said with authority.

Shayna opened her mouth. Closed it, then shook her head. "I'll be fine in a hotel. I mean they have security, and I promise not to open my door for anyone."

Mike sat back looking at the two women. There were so many holes in that scenario, he could drive a diesel through it. Instead of waiting for Greg or Amelia to shut her down, he decided to take the bull by the horns. "Didn't the thief come into your apartment while you were sleeping and steal the other violin? And before you say anything, let me ask you another question. Did you not have your doors locked, because you felt safe in your apartment?"

Again her mouth opened and shut, then she sat back with a dejected look.

"Since I'm assigned to the case, and I have a three bedroom place, which is armed with a security system even the best trained assassin would have a hard time getting past, I suggest she stay with me." Even as the words left his mouth, he thought of being in the same home with the younger woman and hardened. Dozens of cold showers were definitely in his future, not to mention a work out for his left hand. Of course, he was ambidextrous, so his right hand would surely be helping a brother out. The growl bubbling in his gut was barely suppressed.

"I agree with Royce. And since you haven't checked into your hotel, there shouldn't be an issue. Once Pam is finished compiling a list for us, we should have more answers. Until then, you go nowhere alone." Greg's hazel eyes pinned him with a hard stare. The boss man telling him this was more than just an assignment.

Mike didn't need to be told twice. He never failed, and sure as shit this wouldn't be his first with this woman.

The sound of metal scraping against the tile floor had him jerking back to the here and now. Shayna stood looking like a deer in the headlights. "Fine, but we are not locking up my violin, it goes with me."

Spunk. She had that in spades. Well he had a firm hand and wondered if she enjoyed that, then just as quickly suppressed his urges.

"Come on," he said a little too gruffly. "Greg, you got something for her phone in case he calls again?"

A black case was laid out on the table and within minutes Shayna's phone was handed over while Greg did his thing. Mike took the time to properly check her out, not that he hadn't already, but he saw the strain marking her features. The tightness around her eyes and mouth, the stiff set of her jaw and shoulders. Clearly, she had been holding herself together by a thread. She had to have the same core of steel as Amelia. He too stood, coming around the table. "It's going to be okay. I promise, nothing and no one will hurt you as long as you're under my care."

With a jerky nod, she licked her lips. "Amelia said you were one of the best."

He raised a brow, then looked over at the older woman.

"Hey, you're an ex-alphabet member. Obviously you know what you're doing."

"Alright, that should do it. I'll let you know when Pam has some answers. Until then, check in every twenty-four." Greg was a man of very few words.

"Will do." Mike started to reach for her elbow, stopping himself in the nick of time. The last thing he needed was skin on skin contact in front of his bosses when he'd just gotten his body under control.

The two women embraced while he and Greg went over a few key points, all the while he kept his eyes on Shayna.

"She may seem worldly, but she's not." Greg warned Mike.

Tired of feeling like he was a kid being told he wasn't good enough, Mike stood taller, towering over Greg. At six foot three and two hundred and fifty pounds, he didn't easily blend into any crowd, which was why he was usually the one who took the backup position, or bodyguard point in most of he and his old partner Maddox's missions. However, he was not a pussy who took kindly to anyone treating him as if he was less than. "If you want someone else on this job say the word, otherwise back the fuck off."

Greg held both hands up. "Whoa, I'm not saying that. I just know that look. I see it every time I look in the mirror when I'm thinking of Amelia naked."

Heat licked up Mike's insides, but he controlled his outward appearance. "Message heard and received. We'll be sure to report in. You get any intel we should know about, be sure and let me know." He walked around Greg toward the door, deciding it was safer for all if he got some fresh air.

"I'm ready whenever you are."

****

Shayna wasn't sure how she was going to survive the coming days, cooped up under the same roof with the tall drink of water that was Mike Royce. Holy. Hell. The man was sex on a stick. She'd seen the heated exchange between Greg and him, wondering what they'd argued about, but then Amelia had told her not to worry. Now, she couldn't help but hope her drool wasn't showing as he placed a huge hand on her elbow, guiding her out of the warehouse into the bright sunshine.

"I brought my sports car into the office today, but rest assured, it's safe," Mike said, leading her to the sporty little vehicle. He opened the passenger door, then hefted her bright colored bag and sat it into the back before striding around to the driver side.

Her traitorous body did a hallelujah dance as he folded himself into the seat. The denim stretching tight across his thighs did nothing to hide muscles, nor the obvious bulge at the apex. Holy crap on a cracker, the man was huge. Surely he couldn't be much bigger when he was aroused?

"Are you hungry?" His deep voice had her head jerking up in embarrassment, hoping he hadn't caught her staring at his crotch.

"I could use some food." Now that he'd mentioned it, she was starving. Her stomach chose that moment to grumble loudly.

A push of a button had the car starting, the engine rumbling to life. "Anything in particular you like or dislike?"

"I love Mexican, Italian, and Asian. Well, except for seafood, I love all those." She smoothed her damp palms down her thighs drawing his gaze.

His hand went to the gear shift, but his eyes seemed captivated by hers on her thighs. "Then we should get along just fine. I know a great little place we can order some take out Chinese. What do you like?"

She told him, then he had his high tech car call the restaurant. By the time they reached the place, her mouth was watering and her stomach felt like it was eating her backbone.

"They have a drive thru window, which works in our favor." The grin he flashed her had all her girlie parts lighting up like the Fourth of July.

Holy crap. How the heck was this man single, and how was she going to keep from attacking him? Well, she'd never been accused of being a femme fatale, so he was relatively safe.

Mike's home was situated in a private community on Cory Lake. The gate was manned by a guard who made him show his license before large iron gates were opened, making butterflies dance in her stomach.

"What if I want to come and go?" she asked.

Mike shifted gears. "I don't want anyone to know you're here. If someone is tracking you, then entering you into any system could alert them."

The thought had her gut twisting. "So, I'm basically a prisoner until this is over?"

He didn't say anything until they were pulling up to a single level home with terracotta tiles. The beautiful home sat back away from the road and had its own gate that required another code to get into it. "You are not a prisoner, Shayna."

The gates opened, then he accelerated, keeping her from saying another stupid comment. No, she wasn't a prisoner. Someone was stalking her, and he was there to keep whoever from getting their hands on her. Shayna needed to remember he was one of the good guys, and pray Amelia and her team found the bad guys quickly, her next tour was set to start in just over a month. If she wasn't on it, another prodigal violinist would fill her shoes, then what would she do?

Mike pulled into a garage that looked like it came straight out of a showroom. Two other vehicles completely different than the one they were in were parked side-by-side. One a big black pickup that looked like it could drive over the sports car, and the other, an SUV in a pearl white, with a price tag she didn't even want to guess at. Her mind raced to think of what the man had to do to make enough to afford that kind of cash.

"I'll grab your suitcase since you don't like anyone to help you with the violin case. If you want, you can place it in my safe. I can guarantee you, nothing short of a nuclear bomb can get inside it." Mike opened his door before she could respond.

She didn't wait for him to come around and open her door. "I like to have it on hand in case I want to play, or I need to practice."

He stopped in the middle of bending down, then stood, staring at her over the low-slung car. "How much is that one worth, if you don't mind me asking?"

Chewing on her bottom lip, she decided it was better to be honest. "About thirty thousand dollars, give or take a few."

Mike whistled. "That's a lot of cash for an instrument. Wouldn't any violin make the same sound if it was tuned properly?"

Unable to stop herself, she snorted. "After we eat, I'll show you what this one sounds like, then we can pull up someone playing the same song on a violin less superior."

He shrugged, but she'd show him.

"Let's get inside and eat before this gets cold." He held their food in one hand and pulled the suitcase behind in the other. At the door to the interior of the house, he entered another code. Damn, was the man paranoid or what?

"It's better to be safe than sorry," he mentioned looking over his shoulder.

Holding up both hands, she gave him her most innocent look. "Hey, it's working in my favor at the moment."

She expected to walk into a typical man cave, or bachelor pad with a dull black and white motif. The warm and cozy mud room led into a large kitchen, with every appliance a woman would need to make a gourmet meal while her family sat nearby. The colors screamed homey elegance, and the seating invited guests to sit down and relax.

"Take a seat. I'll get us some plates. What would you like to drink? I've got wine, water, and juice." He placed their takeout bag on the counter, then turned toward a cabinet with a glass front.

"Water for me, please."

Once he had two bottles of water and plates out, he took a seat next to her at the counter, then neither of them spoke while they devoured their meals. Shayna sat back with a sigh, exhaustion hitting her hard. A yawn catching her by surprise, making goosebumps break out and causing her to shiver.

"Alright, how about a small tour of the house, and I show you to your room?" Mike finished off his water.

"I'll do the dishes," she protested.

He shook his head. "I have a dishwasher, and you're tired. Next time I'll let you be on clean up duty. Come on." He held out his hand.

At five foot seven, she wasn't used to being short next to men, but with Mike Royce, she felt positively tiny. His large hand waited for hers. She placed her palm in his, instant warmth infused her.

With a tug, he pulled her to stand. "No room is off limits. If you get scared, come find me." Green eyes filled with heat and promise stared down at her.

For a minute she wanted to lean up and beg him to kiss her, but her phone vibrated in her pocket. The interruption made her release his hold. "My mom." She showed him the text. Her mother had learned how to use emojis and was now a huge fan.

He gave a clipped nod, then led the way through his house. The homey feel continued throughout until they reached what was clearly his office. He quickly led her past his own bedroom to the one next door. "Here's your room. It has its own ensuite. You should have all the things you need, but don't hesitate to holler if you want anything."

"I'm just going to take a shower, then hit the bed, where I'm sure I'll sleep for the next twelve hours." She shifted from one foot to the next, waiting for him to leave, or stay and offer to wash her back. Damn, why were her hormones acting like a hussy in heat?

"I'll leave you to it then. If you need me, I'll be in my office just down the hall for the next couple hours." Mike turned on his heel, and strode out, back ramrod straight.

****

Mike didn't think he could stay in her presence for another second, especially not one where a bed was within ten feet of them. His job was to keep her safe, and he was sure she wasn't safe from him stripping her bare just to see if she was as soft as she looked. Nope, he was not going there. No, he didn't need to work another day in his life, his parents had seen to that long before he was born.

However, Mike enjoyed his job. He'd loved working for the government. Covert operations gave him a thrill he'd needed after losing his mom to cancer, followed closely by his dad from a heart attack. As the last Royce in his family, he almost felt it was his duty to do something worthwhile.

An hour ticked by, then another. When he felt it was relatively safe to check on Shayna, he shut down the computers after checking all his alarms were set. He may live in a gated community, but his property backed up to seventeen thousand acres of woodland, which was one of the reasons he couldn't sell the property. He needed to feel close to the outdoors, yet have all the amenities of the city. He was a Miami man through and through. Loved all the night life the city came with. If he'd seen Amelia before Greg had snatched the woman up, he was sure he'd have made a play for the gorgeous Latin woman. However, now that he'd seen Shayna, he couldn't fathom a more beautiful woman. His mind came to a screeching halt. Yes he could, and had. He just couldn't come up with names at the moment.

Shaking off thoughts of women, and focusing on the case instead, one that was clearly not quite so cut and dried, he listened at the closed door next to his own. Reassured she'd fallen asleep, he made his way back to the master bedroom. His body went through the steps of stripping and showering, images of a naked Shayna not a room away had him standing at full attention. "At this rate, I'm going to need more than a cold shower, and a hand job to get through the coming days," he muttered. Flashing green eyes, and a body made for sin appeared in his mind. Mike reached for the body wash on the shelf. Using his hand as a substitute, he worked himself up and down. Forgoing a slow buildup, he imagined what she would feel like sliding up and down his shaft. It didn't take him long before tingles began at the base of his spine, then he was shooting ribbons of come out the tip of his dick. He finished his shower, then dried off, wrapping a towel around his hips. He'd just stepped into his bedroom when he thought he heard a noise in the hall.

Grabbing his gun out of its holster, he went to the door and listened before easing it open a fraction. The sight that met his eyes had him sweating and swearing in equal measures. Shayna walking barefoot down his hallway in a T-shirt and nothing else. But that wasn't what was alarming. No, the fact she didn't seem to be awake was what bothered him. He knew enough about people who sleep walked, and what not to do. She walked into his kitchen, her feet as silent as a wraith. Her hand went to the lock, and as she went to open it, he sat the gun on the counter and put his over hers.

"Shayna, wake up." He kept his tone low.

She blinked a few times, her body going from relaxed to rigid in seconds. "Where am I?"

He would not find her adorable while she rubbed her eyes. Fuck, who was he kidding? "You were walking in your sleep." Mike kept his hand on her much smaller one.

"I haven't done that in years," she said in a sleep roughened voice.

Mike had no reason to continue holding her hand, other than he loved touching her. Yeah, he might really like the feel of her soft skin beneath his, but right now his worry lay at her dainty feet. Feet that had nails painted a vibrant red.

"How about we get you something to drink, and you explain." Mike shuddered at the thought of Shayna walking around a strange city. Hell a strange country.

"I think I'd like that glass of wine now." Her body trembled.

A drink of something much stronger was calling his name. "What kind of wine do you like?"

Her smile when it came lit up her face. "I'd like to say something sophisticated like a Sauvignon Blanc, but I like my wine like I like my coffee, sweet."

"Lucky for you I have what is considered a dessert wine. How about Moscato, is that sweet enough for you?" Mike held a bottle up from his wine fridge.

She gave a happy clap. "Perfect."

He poured her a glass of wine, and him a healthy shot of George Dickel. The amber liquid went down smoothly, a slight burn that he enjoyed. He refilled his glass, watching Shayna sip her own drink. The second drink he savored as he watched her stare into space.

"Alright, so spill. You do that walking around shit a lot?" If she did, he'd need to figure something out about their sleeping arrangements. No way in hell could he rest knowing she might get up at any minute and walk out the door without him being any wiser.

Chapter Three

Shayna rolled her eyes. He made it sound easy. "When I get overly tired I tend to walk in my sleep. Although, I don't think I've ever left my rooms. My parents put alarms on the doors when I was a kid just in case I did happen to walk outside during one of my excursions."

His eyes went to her arms. "You're cold." It was a statement, but the way his eyes looked her up and down, had goosebumps popping up on her body for another reason, other than the cool air.

"I think the wine will help me sleep," she said.

He nodded. "You'll be in my room, that way I'll know if you decide to take a stroll again." He held his hand up. "I'll sleep on the sofa. Your virtue is safe with me."

How was she supposed to tell him she didn't want to be safe with him? Or that he wasn't safe with her. He hadn't put anything on since she'd woke with a start, and seeing him in nothing but a fluffy towel was playing havoc on her female parts. The happy trail disappearing into the terry cloth made her want to rip the offending material away and see if he manscaped, or not. Being the betting gal she was, she'd say definitely manscaped.

"Eyes up here, or I won't be responsible for the tenting of the towel, nor the view you'll be getting." Humor filled his deep voice.

She shook the image of him naked out of her head. "Seriously, Mike, I don't need to sleep in your room. You have alarms on your doors, right?" At his slight nod she continued. "Well there you go. If I happen to step outside your home, then you'll be alerted before I get too far."

A loud sigh came from the frustrating man. "What if someone was lying in wait and got to you before I did?"

Did the man think that was a real possibility? "What's on the agenda for tomorrow?" Maybe if she didn't think about sleeping in his bed…without him, she could get through the night.

"I'll check in with Greg, then take you sightseeing."

Her heart flipped, then took up a fast beat. Never had a man looked at her as if he looked forward to a day spent doing touristy things. Or, she could be seeing things she wanted, when he was only looking forward to a resolution to the situation they were in.

"Alright. I'm ready to go to bed if you are."

She thought she heard him growl something under his breath, but then his face showed nothing other than the mask of a professional. "Lead the way." Mike stepped back and waved his hand for her to go first.

Not wanting to accidentally touch him and make a fool of herself, she made sure to keep a couple feet between them. Inside his room, she inhaled the spicy scent she would always associate with the man. During the home tour he'd given her, she'd only had a glimpse of his bedroom. Now, she padded over to the huge king bed. The side he'd slept on still had a dent from where he'd laid.

Turning around, she faced the object of her desire. "I forgot my violin in my room." She took a step toward the door, stopping when he stepped into her path.

"I'll get it and the rest of your things. I'm assuming you hadn't unpacked yet?" When she shook her head, he gave a clipped nod. "Let me go grab them, and be right back. Make yourself comfortable. Bathroom is through there." He tilted his head toward the open door on the other side of the room.

Licking her lips, she waited until he left before sinking down onto the bed. Once he was out of eyesight, she lifted the pillow to her nose and inhaled. Before he came back and caught her, she put it back and hurried to use the bathroom. Like the bedroom, it was huge, and masculine like the man. Not wanting to look like a bunny boiler, she climbed into the bed on the side he hadn't been using. Good Lord, the man had the most comfy bed in all the world. She sighed as she lay back. Even the pillows felt like she was lying on clouds. Her long flight from Perth, along with the stress of the past weeks, had her falling back to sleep, secure in the knowledge Mike would be there.

****

Mike closed up her suitcase after he'd grabbed all her bathroom supplies. The woman truly was a conundrum. She kept her violin next to the bed as if she didn't want to let it out of her reach even in sleep. He'd almost expected to find it in the bed.

He did a quick once over before turning off the lights and strolling back to his own room. Not sure what he'd expected, but finding his own sleeping beauty wasn't one of them. As quietly as possible, he sat the floral case on the bench at the end of the bed, and the violin next to a sleeping Shayna. Standing over her, he looked down at the dark crescents her eye lashes made on her cheekbones. In sleep she looked even younger than the twenty-eight he knew her to be. At thirty-five, he felt a generation older. Hell, he was a lot older if you went by experience and life lessons.

Glancing at the sofa, he looked longingly at the bed. With a sigh, he grabbed a pillow and the extra blanket from the shelf, then lay down.

He used the remote to turn the lights off, closing his eyes with thoughts of the alluring woman playing in his head. Shit! He needed to think about his nuts in a vice, or seeing his grandparents kissing. Yeah, that's enough to wilt even the stiffest dick.

Morning sunlight streamed in through the French doors across the room, waking him just hours after he fell asleep. Mike stood and stretched, the blanket falling at his feet. He scratched his chest, glaring at the offending sun that woke him. A gasp from the bed had him turning toward it to find Shayna staring wide-eyed at him.

"Um, you might want to cover that." She pointed at him.

He squinted at her, then understanding dawned as he remembered he'd fallen asleep in nothing but the towel last night. Of course, he usually slept in the nude, he'd planned on making an exception for Shayna's benefit. Seeing her gaze still trained on his morning wood he almost put on a little show for her, but being the nice guy he was, he grabbed up the discarded cloth and wrapped it around his waist.

"Sorry about that, it's not my fault though. What's Beyoncé say? *I woke up that way.*" He smiled thinking she would have no clue what he was referring to since she was a lover of classical music and all.

"I'm pretty sure she was meaning her beauty, not the state of arousal." Shayna sniffed, her eyes dancing with mirth.

Mike placed his hands on his hips. "You listen to modern music?"

Sitting up higher in the bed, she crossed her arms over her chest, making his mouth water at the picture she made. For fuckssake, did the woman not realize it wasn't good for his morning wood to be tempting him so?

"I don't only listen to classical if that is what you mean. That is rude of you to put me in a box just because I play a violin. I mean, look at you." She waved a hand at him. "You look like you work out eight hours of the day, but you don't just work out. However, I could think you were just a juice head."

His mind blanked. Yes, he worked out. A lot. He was on missions that required them to be physically fit, and many times they had nothing to do but wait for the marks to make a move, leaving them hours with nothing to do. He wasn't one to sit and do nothing "Point taken. Alright, I'm going to shower in the other bedroom, you can use this one. I'll make us some breakfast, come out whenever you're done."

He strode from the room before he said or did something he might regret. He definitely wasn't going to rub another one out though. Maybe if he refrained from pleasure, he wouldn't want her so much. Didn't eunuchs not want sex after they had their shit clipped?

In the shower across the hall, he pretended his dick didn't exist even though the damn thing was waving like a flag in the wind. The ice cold water helped, making him hurry through the process of showering and shaving.

As he entered the hall, he listened for any sound from his bedroom, cursing the thick door and walls. With a shrug, he strapped his watch in place, checking the smart device for alerts and emails while he walked. Times like these he wished he had a personal chef, then smiled at the thought of another person in his home who would be underfoot. The only time he was comfortable in those situations was when he was cooking the morning after a great night, and that was only if he allowed them to stay the night. Most times his liaisons happened at their place, which made it easier for him to leave. "Wow, I sound like a dick," he muttered.

"You always talk to yourself?" Shayna asked, looking way too alluring for his peace of mind.

He grunted, pulling out the makings for an omelet. "I hope you like omelets, toast, and fruit."

"Sounds great. Can I have a cup of coffee? I'm not human without my morning cup. You're lucky I'm not grunting like you right now." She walked around him, taking a pod out of the holder and putting it into the machine.

Mike kept his next grunt to himself, wishing he'd grabbed a cup of coffee first. Damn, he never did anything without his own strong mug of java. The sound of the machine hissing as it finished Shayna's drink signaled it was his turn. He imagined her voice and the noises she'd make while he fucked her. Grunting would definitely be one of the many sounds, but it wouldn't be because she hadn't had coffee.

"Do you have any cream and sugar?" Her voice came from beside him.

His hands froze in the process of cracking eggs in the bowl. Her tone held a note, he'd bet his next orgasm, she was imagining him the same way. "Cream is in the fridge, and sugar is over there." He motioned to the counter next to where she had been.

Once he had several eggs in the dish, he washed his hands then moved to get his own drink. The sexual tension driving him nuts.

"Need any help?"

Mike took a deep breath, letting it out before he told her exactly how she could help him. "Nope, just have a seat and enjoy the peace and quiet." Hopefully she'd get the hint.

The coffee, when it was done, was a welcome kick to his system. A sigh escaped him as he drank his fill, then went back for another cup. Some thought it was crazy he didn't use a coffeemaker that made coffee by the pot, but he liked the ones with the single serve pods.

"Feeling better?" Shayna smiled from behind her own mug.

He raised a brow. "Are you saying I was a bit of a bear?"

Shayna raised a hand, rocking it back and forth. "Just a wee bit, but I totally get it. I am not all that nice before the liquid gold that is coffee. Of course, I add enough sugar to make it taste like candy, where as I notice you like yours black."

"I like mine a lot of ways, but first thing in the morning, I like it strong." He watched a blush creep up her neck and face, and wondered if she was thinking the same as him. Dirty girl indeed.

"Um, so what are we going to do today?"

He allowed her to change the subject, knowing it was the safest route for them both. "How does a trip down to Miami sound. We can stay the night and visit a friend of mine's club. Do you like to dance?"

Her green eyes lit up. "I love to dance. What kind of club? Please tell me it's a Latin club."

Picturing her moving her body to the beat of any type of music was enough to fire his blood. "Miami Inferno plays all kinds, but yes, they are known for their Latin music as well." He didn't add the little fact about the women go-go dancers.

She looked down at her jeans and off the shoulder shirt. "I'm not really dressed for a nightclub."

"Sweetheart, you look gorgeous." And she did. Her natural beauty would outshine any of the other women in attendance, but he knew women didn't think on the same level. "However, if you want to go shopping when we get there, I don't mind holding your hand, or being your shopping buddy. I will even go into the dressing room with you and help you change. I'm a giver like that." He winked, letting her know he was kidding. However, he could picture her stripping in and out of outfits, and in all honesty, he didn't mind it at all.

"That is so sweet of you." She batted her lashes, smiling like the thought intrigued her.

They ate, and then were loading into his car for the four and a half hour drive down to Miami, with the violin safely tucked into his safe room. He'd assured her nobody could get into the room short of a bomb that would level the entire neighborhood. The pause after his declaration made him think she was still going to insist they bring the instrument, but then she'd nodded, and allowed him to open the room. Yes, that was exactly what she'd done. Allowed him, an ex-CIA operative, a man who was more than twice her size and had killed on more occasions than he liked to think about, but this tiny slip of a woman allowed him to secure a damn violin in his safe room. He snorted.

"What was that?" Shayna asked.

****

The way Mike did everything with an economy of movements was enough to make even a woman who'd been around the world a half a dozen times swoon, and she was not the swooning type. However, she knew that sound he'd just made. Had heard it enough times from men who were not happy with something. If she was to guess, she'd say he was still smarting over her insistence of seeing where her precious Guarius was going to be while they went on their little jaunt.

"Would you like a drink for the road perhaps?" Mike shifted the gear on his sports car instead of answering her.

The flex and play of the muscles in his thigh mesmerized her. He was one big man, but not overkill. Oh no, he was perfect from his head to his feet. Perfectly manicured feet at that. He'd put on a pair of white linen pants and a top in the same material, but the shirt was a coral color that accented his masculinity. The loafers he wore screamed money as well, making her wonder exactly what he'd done before joining the Alpha Team, and if Amelia would tell her his secrets.

"A bottle of water would be great." She tore her eyes away from the expanse of skin exposed at his throat, finding everything about him too handsome.

The gas station he pulled into was just this side of shady, yet he got out without an ounce of trepidation. "Keep the doors locked until I get back."

He didn't have to tell her twice. As soon as the door shut he engaged the locks, and she sat in silence waiting for him to return, hating that she depended on a man for protection. Damn it, why couldn't she be more like Amelia? The confident swagger had men and women alike watching Mike as he made his way back toward the vehicle, the locks popping open.

"Can you teach me the basics in self-defense?" She blurted the question out before she could change her mind.

Mike placed two bottles of Smart Water in the cup holders, then turned to look at her. "Why?"

She shrugged. "I don't like feeling this way."

His assessing gaze took her measure. "I can show you a few things while you're with me."

The breath she'd been holding came out in a loud exhale. "Thank you."

"Don't thank me until after our first session." He fired up the engine, then put his shades on, hiding his eyes from her.

"Is that your way of saying be careful what you ask for, you just might get it?" She crossed her legs.

The charming grin sent a shiver up her spine. "Something like that."

Shayna imitated his grunt, making him bark out a laugh. "I'll take it easy on you," he shifted the gear, then continued. "The first day. After that, all bets are off."

Chapter Four

Mike was glad he had his shades on during the four and a half hour trip. It gave him a chance to study Shayna in the light of day without her seeing. He was sure she wouldn't be as beautiful as he'd thought she'd been the night before. He was wrong, she was even more gorgeous with the sun streaming in, giving her an ethereal look.

He allowed her to choose what they listened to, and was surprised to find her taste in music was as eclectic as his, switching from one station to the next, but never in the middle of a song.

"I'm surprised you like rock as much as you enjoy country. Who is your favorite band?" he asked when they were close to Miami.

She shrugged. "I love a lot of bands and musicians."

He was going to ask her more, but a vehicle swerved in his lane, making him have to take the shoulder, nearly causing a multiple car pileup. "Sonofabitch, hold on, baby." He maneuvered the sports car, uncaring of any damage it may sustain. A glance in his rearview showed there were no accidents and the view in front showed the reckless driver had driven away without a care for the damage he could have caused. "You okay?" His hand automatically reached for hers, which was clenched into a fists.

"Wow, that was close." She nodded.

"Yeah," he agreed. If the other driver would have tried to stick around, he would have thought he'd been trying to run them off the road. As it was, Mike figured it was just a case of someone either texting and driving, or possibly a drunk driving incident. His hand itched to reach for his cell, but then he thought better of it. If he drew attention to them, then whoever was looking for her, may be listening or have someone out looking for her. Decision made, he released her clenched fists.

"How much longer?" Shayna asked.

"About an hour or so. We'll check into a suite, do a little shopping and grab an early dinner, then hit the club." Mike shifted gears, keeping focused on anything but her.

When she said no more, he turned the radio up.

They rolled into Miami a little ahead of schedule thanks in part to his driving, and the fact his riding partner didn't need to stop for a bathroom break every hour. The hotel he chose was an upper level one that had a good security system, plus was close to Miami Inferno.

"Wow, are you expensing this?" Shayna sat up straighter as they waited in the valet line.

He turned his head toward her, then using one finger, he tipped his sunglasses down. "Of course not. I imagine Greg would use the paperwork as basketball practice for his wastepaper basket."

She nodded. "That he would, and then he'd call you up or into the office and rip you a new one."

Mike pushed the glasses back into place. The fact he worked because he wanted to, not because he needed to, was something he didn't share with many.

The valet came to his side, while another opened Shayna's door. Mike barely kept the instinct to growl at the man to back off from escaping. He reached over, grabbing Shayna's arm. "Wait by the side of the car for me," he said too low for the others to hear, then quickly exited.

Shayna grabbed her purse, while he grabbed his overnight bag and the small case she'd brought. He held his hand out, his look daring her. They were supposed to be a couple on holiday he'd explained on the drive. The little minx smiled up at him, then instead of grabbing his hand, her arm snaked around his waist, snuggling into him.

He bent, putting his lips next to her ear. "Be good, or I'll spank that pert little ass of yours."

She licked her lips. "Now that sounds fun."

A groan, part lust fueled, part fear she was playing with him, bubbled out of his clenched teeth. "Oh it will be much more than fun." He let his hand trail down her rear, giving it a little tap.

Her hand trailed down his back, feathering over his ass. "Promises, promises."

In that moment he wanted to say screw shopping and dinner. He wanted to whisk her up to the suite he'd reserved under an alias, but then common sense prevailed. "Put a pin in this convo and we will return to it later." That was most definitely a promise he'd love to keep.

They entered the upscale hotel with him keeping a firm hold on Shayna. His arm now locked around her waist. Not once did she try to move away.

Once they were given the keys and he waved the bellhop away, he and Shayna walked arm and arm toward the bank of elevators. "Are you hungry or would you like to shop first?"

At his question, she sighed. "I hate shopping. I usually just grab something that's in the window display, figuring the sales people clearly know more than me and I'm good to go."

"Well, luckily for you, I happen to have a keen eye for fashion." Mike held the door to their rooms open. He made a quick sweep of the space, then sat his suitcase in one of the rooms, placing hers in the other, then realizing she had a penchant for sleepwalking, he retraced his steps. "You'll be sleeping in here with me. We can build a wall between us with pillows."

"Has that worked with previous lady friends?" she asked walking to look out the bank of windows.

His instincts screamed at him to make her move back away from the glass, but he moved next to her instead. "Nope, I've never had to."

"I bet. So, we doing this or not?" Nervousness edged her voice.

Mike turned her to face him, the sun cast a glow around her. "What's wrong?"

She shrugged. "I don't want to embarrass you."

Confusion made him frown. "How would you do that?"

"I'm not like the women you probably have brought here before. I don't like to shop. I don't have the confidence to just hop into bed with you, even though I play at it. And…I can't dance." She tried to step away.

He gripped her upper arms. "First of all, shopping is not a big deal. You're a rare treasure, and it will be my pleasure to show you the joy of going into a boutique and finding a dress. Second, I never expected you to hop into bed with me. This is a job, and even though I find you one of the most gorgeous women I've had the pleasure of meeting, it isn't part of the requirements of being with me to hop into bed as you put it. And last, but certainly not least…how can you not dance if you play music, and I thought you said you liked Latin dancing. Besides, the beat is in you, you just haven't figured out how to make your body flow with it. Luckily for you, I'm a great teacher. Now, do you need to use the ladies room before we head out?"

Shayna shook her head, then a beautiful smile lit her face. "You're truly full of shit, but I thank you for your words. As for liking Latin dancing, I do. I love to watch it done by those who can do it, and do it well. I just happen to not be one of them." Then she stood on her toes and kissed his chin.

Mike stood stunned for all of two seconds, but having hold of her arms, he didn't allow her to step away. "I'm not lying. In fact, every word that just came out of my mouth is factual. However, instead of trying to convince you with words, I'll do it with actions. Well, all except the second one. If I made love to you, we'd be here for hours and miss shopping, eating and dancing." He grinned at her open mouthed expression. "Hold that thought. I need to check in with Greg first."

****

Shayna searched his face, yet could tell he really believed what he said. The man was probably one of the sexiest she'd ever seen, and she had been around some of the most alluring in the world.

She'd played the violin for princes, and kings. Yet this man could cause her to be speechless. The feel of his hard body pressed against hers, had her thinking of all the things she'd like to experience. She knew without a doubt he would be a wonderful lover, unlike the last man she'd been with. Lord, that man didn't even deserve to be called a lover. Two minute man at best.

"Alright, but I'm holding you to it. You make me look stupid, and I'm going to find a way to repay you in kind." She poked his chest with her finger, the warmth of his skin radiating out.

"I guess I'm safe then. Unless we stay here, and then neither of us are safe. I need to check in with Greg before we do anything though," he growled.

He released his hold on her, stepping away reluctantly, or was that her wishful thinking? His voice muted as he spoke with Greg, yet she saw him glance at her over his shoulder, heat licking at her like he was physically touching her. Shit, she was in so much trouble.

When he placed the phone back in his pocket she waited for him to face her. "What did Greg say?"

Mike didn't seem to be stunned at her question. "They are still getting Intel in, but said we should be on high alert," he answered honestly.

In minutes they were back out in the heat of Miami and entering a boutique she was sure would cost a mint. True to his word, Mike found a dress that she never would have thought to purchase for herself. Having red hair, a yellow dress would have been so far from one she'd have thought to try on. Now, she stood in the dressing room, staring at herself in the mirror as if she'd never seen the woman staring back at her.

She recalled his words as he'd handed her the form fitting dress, saying it reminded him of the sweetest lemonade and made him thirsty. She wondered if he'd still think the same once he saw her in it.

A pair of white strappy heels appeared over the door. "Here, try these on with the dress, and hurry up. Surely you have the dress on by now?"

Rolling her eyes, she slid the shoes on, amazed when they fit. "How did you know my size?" she asked the man standing outside the closed door.

"It's my job to be observant, and believe me, I've observed everything about you." The deep timber of his words sent a shiver of need down her spine.

An image of him standing naked in the morning sunlight popped into her head. The man was glorious in his nudity, and hung like no other she'd seen outside of magazines. "Oh, I've observed too, dear man."

"Got quite an eyeful, huh?" He didn't sound the least bit embarrassed.

Knowing when to give up, she unlocked the door, took a deep breath and stepped out. Mike whistled.

"Damn, you look better than I thought you would. Turn around." He made a spinning motion with his finger.

She felt like a model, and instead of disobeying, she did as asked, doing a slow spin to keep from tottering on the high heels.

"Oh, that looks fabulous. Do you need some accessories to go with it?" A sales girl interrupted them.

Shayna blinked, then shook her head. She had plenty of jewelry, just none with her. "No thank you. I'll just take the dress and shoes."

"Can you snip the tags off? She's going to wear the outfit out of here and place her clothes in the bag." Mike spoke over Shayna's protests.

The sales girl looked between them, then nodded. "Absolutely, let me get a pair of scissors."

"Don't argue. This way we can go straight to dinner and not have to go back to the hotel. This boutique will deliver your old clothes to the hotel as well. It's called full service for a reason, love." He stepped into her space, using his finger to tilt her face up to his. "Can I just tell you how sexy you look in that dress?"

Her breath froze in her throat.

"Here we go." They were interrupted again by the young girl, who if Shayna didn't know better, she'd think the woman had a thing for Mike. Of course, the man was built like a freaking god.

"Thank you, Therese. Could you please have these delivered to our hotel?" He rattled off the name of the place they were staying.

Once they were out on the sidewalk again, Shayna gripped her new bag Mike insisted she needed in order to match her dress. "Was Therese an ex-girlfriend or something?" Too late she realized jealousy dripped from her voice.

Mike stopped in his tracks. "Hell no. I'd never met her before today." A smile split his face. "Are you jealous?"

She tried to turn away from his knowing grin.

"Ah, you have no reason. Since I saw you, there hasn't been another woman who could compare."

Again, truth rang out. "I'm being stupid. You don't owe me any explanations or...anything. I'm just a job. A mission to you."

"You're right, of course." Mike nodded, his jaw bunched. "Let's eat, I'm starved."

Shayna heard hurt in his tone, but when she looked at him, the smiling man was looking at her, waiting for her to agree. "Me, too. I think I could eat an entire pot of spaghetti."

"Well, then I guess it's Italian, and lucky for you I made reservations." He didn't take her hand, or put his arm around her as they walked, and she felt the loss. Although she couldn't fault his protective stance as he stayed close with his body on one side, and the building on the other.

He made dinner an act of torture. Torture for her because he used the pasta swirled on his fork like it was an act of sex. His tongue would come out, and he'd place the bit of food on it, making her all too aware of the things he could do with that bit of his anatomy. Her eyes narrowed on his, thinking two could play that game. She lifted a meatball from her plate, nibbled on it, licked some of the marina off before popping the meat into her mouth and moaned. "Oh man, this is delicious. You truly do have the best taste," she said after she swallowed.

His eyes darkened, his throat worked up and down. "Yeah, it's great," he croaked.

Score one for her, Shayna silently cheered. The rest of the meal finished without either of them tasting it she was sure, but the heated glances he gave her let her know she had affected him the same as he had her. After he paid the bill, he shocked her by standing then pulling out her chair. The man was a complete conundrum, one she was only beginning to realize would take her years to figure out.

"You ready to dance some of these calories off?" Mike asked, leading the way out the door of the restaurant.

Shayna shook her head. "I told you I can't dance. I like to people watch and listen to the music. I can literally listen to almost any song and then play it on just about any instrument, but when it comes to the dancing part, I have two left feet."

They walked hand in hand down the busy sidewalk toward his friend's club, aptly named Club Inferno since it was hotter than Hell in Miami most days.

A groan left her lips at the sight of the long line of people waiting to get in. "I hate waiting in lines," she muttered.

Mike gave her hand a gentle squeeze. "Trust me, love. There will be no wait." His cocky grin had her heart somersaulting. Passing the line of men and women, dressed from scantily clad bits of nothing, to high end fashion, he walked up to a man holding a clip board.

The tall man dressed in a black tailored suit cocked his head to the side, and checked his list for Mike's name. Once they were cleared, he undid the red velvet rope and let them pass, much to the dismay of the people in line.

Inside, she paused at the sight that met her eyes. Here was clearly where the gorgeous people went to party. Wall to wall gorgeous men and women either stood or sat in groups that looked straight out of GQ.

"Come on, we'll head to the table and order a drink there." Mike's reassuring arm around her waist steered her through the crowd.

Shayna wasn't sure what she'd expected, but the opulence of the club was different than any she'd been to. Girls dancing in little cages wearing outfits she'd never pull off. Up the stairs they climbed to a section that was obviously reserved for the more important or wealthier clients. Again, she was stunned when Mike was greeted by one of the most handsome men she had ever seen.

"Royce, you crazy devil. When did you get into town?" A tall dark haired man stood up and greeted them, pulling Mike into a hug.

Shayna stared between the two men. Both tall and gorgeous.

A petite woman came up behind them. "Hi, my name is Angelina, but people call me Angel."

She shook the other woman's hand, confidence radiating from the firm grip. "Hi, I'm Shayna."

At five foot seven she felt positively huge next to the tiny woman who couldn't be more than a little over five foot herself.

Introductions were made around the sitting area that looked more like a high end living room. The owner, Lorenzo Delgado and his fiancée Angelina Rugiero, were longtime friends of Mike's, yet she couldn't fathom how he knew such wealthy people.

"Would you like something to drink, bella?" Lorenzo asked, holding a bottle of Champagne over a crystal flute.

"Yes please." She held the stem of the glass while the golden liquid was poured. All around them music played while people danced or talked. Having been to many venues around the world, she relaxed and let herself enjoy the delicious drink. Obviously the Cuban man didn't skimp on the expensive alcohol.

"So, what brings you to my city, Royce?" Lorenzo lounged back, one arm behind his fiancée.

Mike shrugged. "I wanted to show Shayna the nightlife in Miami since she was back in the states. She plays the classical violin."

Her eyes shot to his at the sound of pride in his voice.

"You play in an orchestra?"

At Lorenzo's question, she sat the now empty flute down. "I have, and do on occasion, but mostly I play solo." When he raised one dark eyebrow, she explained.

Watching as his fingers trailed along Angel's bare arm, Shayna felt a bit jealous at the easy affection and missed what he said next. "I'm sorry, can you repeat that?"

"Do you play other instruments?" Lorenzo smiled with a knowing grin.

Mike leaned in close, setting his lips next to her ear. "He is very much in love with his fiancée."

The anger behind his growled words, too low for anyone but her to hear had her turning to meet the burning glare. "I wasn't...I don't," she stammered. "Excuse me, I need to use the ladies room." She moved off of the small loveseat.

"I'll go with you," Angel said.

Two large men who looked more like mafia hitmen moved in close.

"They will not be alone my friend. Stay and chat with me." Lorenzo waved a hand at the men.

Shayna rolled her eyes, but looked back at Mike for his reassurance.

"Stay with Angelina," he warned.

"We'll be using the restroom in Lorenzo's office down the hall instead of the one downstairs. It'll only take us a moment, no worries." She smiled.

Shayna swore the other woman had to be part goddess, part true angel.

The door they came to had a security pad that required a code, then the thick door swung open. Inside, Shayna wasn't surprised to see more opulence, or a huge desk that looked straight out of the eighteenth century. "Is your fiancé a mobster or what?" She blurted. Never had she been accused as a foot in mouth type of woman, but she could be forgiven in some circumstances.

Angel laughed. "You'd think that, huh? But, the answer is no. He's dreamy, and sexy as all get out, but everything about him is legal. Hell, he wouldn't even touch me until he was one hundred percent sure I was of age, and lived a full life," she growled the last bit.

"I'm sure there is a story there somewhere?" Her body was letting her know the need to visit the ladies room wasn't a ruse, but a real need.

"Why don't you use the little girls room? I'll wait out here." Angel opened a door off to the side of the large room.

She tried not to gape, but seriously, the man must be loaded. Who the hell has a shower made for two in an office bathroom, along with a closet and all things necessary like a home bathroom? Not wanting to appear as if she'd snooped around, she quickly finished and washed her hands.

Angel leaned on the massive desk, looking at her phone. "Alright, now spill. How did you meet Mike Royce? I've only seen him a few times with Ren, and he was super secretive. Like a super spy, James Bond type. If I hadn't always been head-over-ass in love with Lorenzo, I'd have totally been in lust with that huge hunk of man." Angel winked.

Shayna relaxed, knowing the younger girl didn't actually have her sights on Mike, nor was she being intrusive. The only problem was, she couldn't tell her too much. "Well, I've known men like him my entire life." She shrugged, hiding the hurt behind honesty. "I don't think I'm really his type, you see. I'm sure you've seen his usual type of woman and I'm thinking I don't quite measure up. You know." Shayna raised her right arm, then mimicked with both. "Tall, blonde and stacked. Not to mention, I do have a brain in my head, and happen to disagree with a lot of what he says." They both laughed.

With a nod, Angel pushed away from the desk. "If you don't really know him, I wouldn't make assumptions. You don't want to miss out on a good man, I can tell you from experience it sucks to watch someone you care about walk away from you." She patted Shayna on the arm. "I'm going to use the restroom while we're here. Lord knows Ren hates when I leave his side too many times. Just hang out here, and feel free to make yourself a drink if you want."

The bar off to the side looked fully stocked, but she couldn't fathom helping herself. A vibration on top of Lorenzo's desk had her looking to see Angel had left her phone on it, but Shayna didn't look to see who was texting or calling, whichever the case may be. Moments later, Angel reappeared, smoothing the skirt of her expensive dress.

"Your phone was buzzing, but I don't know if it was a text or call."

"Shit!" Angel hurried over to the desk. "God that man is a pain in my butt." She turned away, tapping on her phone, although she didn't seem to mind if her tone of voice was any indication as she read her texts.

To give Angel a modicum of privacy, she went to the bank of windows overlooking the Miami strip. Shayna was normally a very confident person, but Angel was miles above her in that department. The dress the small Latin woman wore showed off her curvy figure to perfection. She had no doubt, Ren had his hands full in more than one sense of the word.

A sigh had her focusing on Angel.

"He is so lucky I love him to distraction." Smiling, Angel held the pink phone to her chest. "Are you ready to return? Ren has promised they are ready to dance."

Horrified at the thought of making a fool of herself, she shook her head. "Um, I think I'll just watch."

"Oh, no. We shall dance, girlfriend. Our men love to dance, and it is the best form of torture." Her extremely long lashes came down, then up in an exaggerated wink. "Follow my lead, and trust me. Mike and Ren can out dance any man on that floor."

Her heart beat double time. If she was to admit she had two left feet, would Angel laugh at her? The other girl grabbed her hand and before she knew what was happening they were walking out the door and into the waiting arms of Ren. Well, Angel was. Mike stood with his arms crossed as if he'd gotten as impatient as Angel's fiancé. Lord, but the man looked too damn good scowling down at her.

"I guess we are dancing." He unfolded his arms, moving into her space.

She went up on her toes. "I cannot dance remember?"

His own head bent, brushing his mouth across hers. "And I can, so it will be fine. I'll lead, while you follow. Trust me. "

Those two little words made her head spin, and her heart stop and start again. She licked her lips, then did the craziest thing. She nodded and let him steer her toward the stairs and then down to the crowded dance floor.

Chapter Five

Mike kept the fist pump to himself as Shayna agreed to dance with him. She may think she couldn't dance, but anyone who could play a musical instrument had rhythm in their soul. His friend Ren led Angel onto the dance floor. The crowd seeing the couple enter opened up, leaving a huge space for them to perform. Mike realized the pair were obviously well known for being more than just the owner and his gorgeous woman. Just then the DJ started playing a popular song that had him pulling Shayna in close to his body, and he forgot all about Ren and everyone else.

"Relax, let your body move with mine." He held her left hand in his right, while he smoothed his other palm along her hip. "Feel the beat vibrating along the floor?" He brought their combined hands between their bodies and rested it above her heart.

"You can feel it here as well. Let yourself enjoy the beat, and let me lead our bodies."

Her heart beat faster than the music, but her body melted against his and then she was letting him lead her across the floor. Were they the best dancers? No. But, she was smiling, and his own body was reacting to the feel of hers as he pulled her close, and held her, or swayed to the music. As one song led to the next, he realized she was the most naturally honest woman he'd ever met.

"This is so fun," she breathed out, eyes sparkling up at him after the last song finished. Mike loved to dance and had danced with women who could move like professionals, but none held a candle to Shayna.

A slow number began, one that brought her flush with him. He'd lost sight of Ren and Angel, but the other couple along with all others had ceased to exist once he'd had the gorgeous Shayna in his arms. "Yeah." The one word was said on a groan. Her arms came up and around his neck. At six foot three, he towered over her normally smaller frame of five foot seven, but in her heels, she was much closer to his height, making it easier for him to look down into her upturned face. He imagined closing the small distance to her mouth and seeing if she tasted as sweet as she looked. He wanted to see what she'd chosen to wear under the dress they'd picked out. His hands itched to lift the hem, and find out for himself if she was as soft all over as she was where he'd already touched. His dick had been hard as stone since the first dance.

"Mike, I," she stuttered as a body knocked into her from behind.

In a blink he went from horny, to instantly alert. They were in the middle of a crowded dance floor where a killer could be, and he was thinking of completely inappropriate thoughts. *Real smooth, Royce.* "You ready to take a break?" He asked, steering them off the dance floor and away from so many unknowns.

Shayna blinked gorgeous green eyes. Damn! Everything about the woman was perfect and way too alluring for his peace of mind.

"Actually, I'm thirsty and more than a bit tired." A yawn cracked her jaw.

He lifted his hand, running the knuckles of his fingers down her cheek. Smooth skin tempted him. "Let's go find Ren and Angel to let them know we're leaving."

As they were heading up the stairs Mike felt the hair on the back of his neck raise. His body reacted by pulling Shayna closer to him, placing her next to the wall with him blocking her from wherever the danger could be. Looking to the left and right, he scanned the crowd, but too many people milled back and forth.

"You're scaring me, Mike." Her hands clenched in the material of his shirt.

He reached back with his left arm, trying to reassure her. "I'm sorry. I always listen to my instincts, and they're screaming at me right now." A waitress with a tray full of drinks was walking toward the table where he knew Ren and Angel were probably sitting. Before she walked past them, he used her as a shield, hating himself for putting either woman in danger, but figured if there was a possible threat, they wouldn't take out an innocent. He hoped.

Ren sat with Angel in his lap and two other couples grouped around them. Before they reached them, his friend looked up, the smile disappearing instantly. He sat Angel down as he rose.

"What is it?" Ren asked immediately.

Mike shook his head, knowing his longtime friend would offer assistance without question. "I need an escape route that is not out the front, and one that someone can't follow."

"Derek, watch the women. Angel, stay here and don't argue." He bent and kissed Angel silencing her, then moved to stand on the other side of Shayna. "Follow me." He snapped his fingers, several men took up position from the surrounding area stepping closer. Ren gave the men orders, then two followed as they strode through the crowd and back toward the office.

Knowing his friend and the wealth he had, Mike didn't question the amount of security nor the fact they were so discreet. In that moment, he needed every advantage. Why he'd thought coming to Miami was a good idea, he had no clue. Of course, he could be overreacting. But, he'd been in the business long enough to know to trust his instincts and his were screaming. They formed a wall around Shayna, while he kept her close to his left side where he could reach his weapon if needed, the slight shaking she couldn't hide ate at him.

"Don't worry, I'll get you out of here," he whispered next to her ear.

Startled green eyes gazed up at him.

She bit into her lower lip. "I don't know why this is happening to me."

There was a reason, he just needed to figure out why before whoever was out to get her succeeded. Not on his watch he vowed.

He'd been inside Ren's club and office before, but never had he needed to use any exit other than the front, or back door of the club. Yet, he should have known the other man would have an emergency exit there as well. They didn't speak until the door was closed behind the five of them, with the two guards standing inside the door.

Ren turned in the middle of the room, pinning him with his dark stare. "Want to tell me what's going on, Royce?"

Shayna's body stiffened. Mike trusted Ren, but the less he knew the safer for all of them. Sighing he shook his head. "I thank you for your help, but trust me when I say it's best for all if you don't know. I didn't mean to bring trouble to your club."

The big Latin man folded his arms across his chest, then a slight curve of his lips followed. "If it has to do with the woman you can't seem to let go of, then I understand." He held up his hand. "Trust me, I have felt what you are going through when I nearly killed Angel's ex," he growled. "I'll take you down to the private garage that only my family and I have access to. You can use one of my cars, or one of my men can drive you, whatever you choose."

Mike released Shayna, and went over to Ren. "You are a true friend. I won't forget this."

"I owe you still." Lorenzo Delgado was a man who loved his family, and when his little brother's girlfriend had died, the younger man had fallen into drugs. Mike had been the one to find Fernando Delgado on the brink of death and was able to save him, but he'd have done it for anyone, especially for his friend's baby brother.

"I won't argue with you since it is a waste of breath. Stay sharp, and don't let Angel out of your sights. Alert Gia as well." He knew the only female of the Delgado's was the princess of the family and was usually at the club with her best friend Angel.

"I already had Derek take care of that," Ren agreed.

He breathed a sigh, then held his hand out. "Thank you my friend. It was great seeing you and Angel again. I'm glad you finally got your head out of your ass where she was concerned."

The smile that lit Ren's face was blinding when it came. "I'm a lucky man indeed. Now, you better come to the wedding." He gave the date and time, waiting until Mike put it into his calendar.

"We better go. Thank you again." Mike was pulled into a hug, knowing his friend truly did feel he owed him made him feel as if his life was worth more than the next job. He looked back to see Shayna watching them. He cleared his throat.

Ren chuckled. "Ah, this one, he has problem showing his feelings. My Angel, she has shown me the error of my ways." He winked, then walked them over to the wall, showing the hidden door and led them down to the garage.

Mike pushed them behind him, drawing out his Glock. "Stay behind me. Both of you," he ordered. The two bodyguards moved with him, making a sweep of the area. They checked the vehicles, making sure they were safe.

"Do you and Angel prefer a certain vehicle?" Mike looked around before turning to question Ren.

With a shake of his dark head, Ren waved his hand. "Take any one you choose. I'll have one of my men retrieve it from your hotel."

After another backslapping hug, he and Shayna took the least obvious vehicle, which was a

Mercedes with tinted windows, and the only one that wasn't a convertible.

"I really liked him. He was not what I'd expect from someone so rich." Shayna smoothed her hands on her skirt.

Knowing the action was from nerves, he reached over and took her fingers into his, bringing them to his mouth and placing a kiss on the tips. Her breath hitched. He moved their hands to his thigh and left them there while he drove around Miami. The Mercedes was an automatic, which he was happy for as he didn't have to release her hand in order to shift. They drove around for a half hour, while he made sure they weren't being followed. He kept up a steady conversation, hoping to relax Shayna. Her humor shone in her easy replies to the topics they talked about, making him laugh out loud, something he hadn't done in too long.

"You actually saw someone throw up in a tuba? And then he went on to play in front of thousands of people?" They were heading back towards their hotel with the windows up, the air conditioning running on low when he saw her shiver. He hated to release her hand, but he shrugged out of his jacket, and handed it to her.

"Oh! Thank you." She smiled, moving around to place it over her arms.

"You're most welcome."

****

Shayna couldn't believe how comfortable she was with Mike. Telling him about the incident with the tuba, she couldn't help but laugh. The poor guy had been embarrassed, but he'd been a trooper.

"Well, did he?" Mike asked again.

"Yeah, he did. After he dumped the contents in a large trash can and one of the stage managers helped him clean it. I figured there was nothing I could do after that that would be on that level. Whenever I go on stage, I picture his green face, and it helps steady me." Except tonight when she realized Mike was on edge.

Her hands fisted in her lap.

"Hey, I won't let anything happen to you." Mike's warm hand reached for hers.

She loved having her hand rest on his thigh the entire trip. When he'd noticed her shivering, she'd cursed herself for being cold, and wished she could have been brave enough to put her hand back. Now, his warm palm was on her thigh. Close to her skin, but not close enough. What kind of woman was she to want a man who she just met, yet wanted with every fiber of her being?

"Are you hungry?" Mike asked.

Her face flamed, thinking he'd read her mind, then she realized they were nearing the hotel. "Um, no," she stammered.

His fingers tightened on hers. "When we get to the hotel, I want you to wait for me to come around. Don't let the valet help you out, okay?"

Licking her lips, she nodded and swore she heard him groan.

There was a line of cars vying to get into the hotel, but Mike maneuvered around them, and up to the front, something she'd never have had the nerve to do. Luckily, none of the valets came to her door or Mike's. He strode around, holding her door open while acting as a shield. Not once did she feel the least bit afraid. This man who she just met, made her feel as if he would hold the world up with one arm, while he held her with the other. The thought had her reaching for his hand he held out.

She held his jacket out for him so he could hide his gun, which he quickly slipped on, then they made their way into the hotel. He made sure the vehicle was locked, and passed the keys to the valet saying who would be picking up the car. The way the young man's eyes lit up at the mention of Lorenzo Delgado's name, she'd swear Mike had mentioned royalty.

At the elevator, Mike made sure she stood in front of him while they waited for the doors to open. She looked over her shoulder and up into his green eyes. "So, is Lorenzo like some big thing here in Miami or what?"

His lips quirked up. "He thinks he is." He paused as the doors opened, then walked them forward. They were the only two who entered. "I think the rest of Miami probably thinks so too."

As he explained that the Delgados were mega-rich, she almost felt faint, but then, she'd played for kings and queens. She'd just never been friends with them like Mike.

"He's a great guy. I met him and his best friend Derek years ago and have stayed in contact with them both over the years. Now, enough about them," he muttered.

Again, before she could say anything the doors opened on their floor. Mike was moving out before her, clearing the way for them. Or rather for her. The man took his job of protecting her seriously.

"It's clear. Come on." Mike reached back for her hand. She noticed he was always touching her in some way. An arm around her waist. His hand in hers. His body against hers. Something most would think nothing about, yet she had felt all the way to her core.

Once they reached the suite he'd rented, she held her hand up. "I'll wait right here while you make sure it's secure, sir," she said impishly.

He shook his head. "No, you'll come in and wait by the door." He brushed his lips over hers.

Shayna gasped, the slight contact sent a thrill all the way to her toes. Holy shite as her ancestors would say.

"Okay, let's go." Mike held their bags in one hand.

She snapped out of her daze. "What?"

"If whoever was following us has found us, then more than likely they also know which room we rented. I always have a plan B."

His grin was devastating and she trusted him implicitly. Without questioning him, she let him lead her out of the room after he made sure the way was clear. They didn't take the elevator like she'd thought, but the stairwell. He pulled out his phone, tapped a few keys, then they went up a few flights where he typed into his phone again. Her shoes were not made to walk up several flights of concrete stairs, but she didn't complain.

"You doing okay? Need me to carry you?"

Heat licked her belly at the thought of him holding her close, but she shook her head. "I'm fine," she lied.

Finally, they stopped after a few more flights up. "He looked at his phone and they had to have a special code to enter the level they were on. Whatever he did, he clearly had connections, or had hacked the hotel. The red light turned green, and then they were walking through as if they were allowed.

The other floor had carpet, but this one had a white marble look that her heels clacked on, making her flinch with each clack.

"This is it," Mike announced.

This time he didn't need to tell her to wait inside the door while he did his walk through, gun in hand.

Her body felt strung as tight as one of the strings on her violins. God, she hated this.

A tear she'd fought hard to hold back escaped. Time held no meaning. She didn't know how long it took Mike to search the suite. It was much larger looking than the one they'd left. Minutes passed, and she just wanted to fall into a heap and cry.

"Hey, it's going to be okay." Mike caught her chin in his hand.

She hadn't realized he'd returned. Bringing her hand up, she tried to wipe away the wetness, but he beat her to it, smoothing away the tracks with his thumbs. He then completely undid her as he gathered her close to his chest. "Go ahead, let it all out." His deep voice and soothing hand running up and down her back was the last straw. She'd stayed strong for too long. Great wracking sobs finally came out. Shayna was not a crying sort, but when she did, they were not the pretty sort. By the time she finished, she knew she was a hot mess, and that her makeup had to be ruined. Yet Mike held her, murmuring comforting words while his big arms held her against him. Then she realized they were no longer in the hallway, nor was she standing on her own two feet.

"Feel better now?" He let her pull back, and she could see her black mascara staining his shirt.

"I must look a mess, and so are you." She touched the wetness on him, feeling the hard body beneath.

He used his forefinger to lift her face up to meet his eyes. "It's nothing. I asked you a question."

Amazingly, she did feel better. Not even a slight headache from her crying jag. She nodded.

"Good, then you can ruin as many of my shirts as you like."

His smile was devastating. They were seated on a long sofa in an elegant living room with the lights down low. She took the time to look around, and noticed there was a piano in one corner and a few more musical instruments on stands as well. She gasped at the sight. "What the heck?" Her mouth flew open in shock.

Mike chuckled. "I finagled the Mozart room. Plan B."

He looked way too smug, but she was too stunned to say anything. The longer she sat there, the more aware she became of several things. One, she was sitting across the most gorgeous and generous man she had ever met. Two, her dress had ridden up so high, she was almost showing her panties. Three, Mike was beginning to get aroused. Four, so was she.

"I should go wash my face," she mumbled.

"Alright. Let me help you up." Mike stood with her in his arms.

God, but he was not only strong, but a gentleman. She was easily losing her heart to a man who was being paid to protect her. Fool, she silently chastised herself.

She took a few extra minutes to wash and dry her face and used the facilities, then staring at her freshly cleaned face, Shayna pressed her hands against the cool marble. "Don't think too hard, girl. Take what you can. Live for today, for tomorrow is not a guarantee." Those were words she'd heard from a very wise woman. Her Nana had told her on more than one occasion how precious life was. With those words fresh in her mind she rolled her shoulders, head held high, she opened the door, nearly colliding with Mike.

"I was just coming to make sure you hadn't fallen in." He had his hands in his pockets, looking too sexy for her peace of mind.

"Oh, I was just making sure I got all the makeup off." Which was true to an extent.

He nodded. "You hungry or thirsty?"

"I could use a drink." At the mention of a drink, she felt parched.

Mike led her over to a mini bar. She took a bottle of water, while he did the same.

"Would you play me something?" He indicated the instruments.

Her fingers itched to pick up the violin even though it wasn't her beloved Guarius, or the stolen Stradivarius. "Sure, do you have any requests?"

"Surprise me. Play one of your favorites." He sat across from where the instrument in question was resting.

Shayna knew he thought she'd play a classical piece, and wanted to show him she enjoyed more than just Mozart, or Beethoven. However, she started with one that most everyone would have recognized. Eine Kleine Nachtmusik Serenade No. 13 by Wolfgang Amadeus Mozart. The German title means a little serenade, or more accurately translated as a little night music.

She relaxed her muscles when she finished, and he looked genuinely awed. Then she put the violin back up to her shoulder, knowing he expected her to play another classical piece.

Grabbing the remote, she scrolled through the playlist until she found the one she wanted, then when the music began, she started. Not once did she look up, letting the heavy throb of Metallica's song One flow through her. As the last note played, she breathed out then chanced a glance to see how he'd reacted.

Mike stood, and walked toward her. "That was amazing." He carefully took the violin from her, setting it back in its holder gently, then took her mouth in a heated kiss, stealing her breath, and her sanity.

He'd shed his coat and the first few buttons of his shirt were undone. She could smell the clean musky scent that was all Mike, all male. His strength and warmth called to her, enveloped her in a sense of comfort that melted any restraint. *Tomorrow isn't guaranteed.* The words echoed in her mind. She was going to take what she could, whatever the consequences to her heart, for she knew Mike was not a forever man, but he would be a wonderful lover. Of that she had no doubt.

"Make love to me, Mike." She broke away from the kiss.

Her heart stopped while she waited for him to decide. Maybe calling it making love was the wrong thing. For her, she feared her little organ pumping blood through her veins had already claimed him, but she'd keep that news to herself.

"Are you sure? Be very sure, Sile," he groaned.

Hearing him call her the Irish word for musical or pure, she stood on her toes, and kissed him, fiercely, leaving no doubt to either of them.

Chapter Six

Mike swept Shayna into his arms. He'd known she was a talented musician. Hell, no way would she be playing a multimillion dollar instrument on loan if she wasn't. However, he was blown away as she played for him. Yes, he had heard Mozart many times, but when she played along with one of heavy metals greatest bands in his opinion, his mind was blown. The woman was unlike any he had ever known. Innocence wrapped in lace and silk.

Once in the largest bedroom, he placed her on her feet next to the side of the bed. "Are you sure?" He needed her, but he wouldn't take advantage of her or the situation.

Her nimble fingers lifted to the buttons of his shirt and began undoing them the same as she did him. If he'd been a better man, he would have stopped her and told her to wait until the light of day. Hell, who was he kidding, he didn't think he could have done it even then. He'd wanted her from the first moment he'd seen her.

"Mike, I am surer of this and wanting you, than I am of anything else. Now, do you want me is the million dollar question?"

He bent and stopped her question with a kiss. Fuck, he was harder than he'd ever been in his thirty-five years. The feel of her hands were different than any other. The pads of her fingers had small calluses from years of playing the violin, and he wondered what they'd feel like stroking him.

Before he could come like a teenager on his first go, he used his own hands to divest her of the dress, finding the hidden zip in the side. Once she was down to the little scraps of silk and lace, his own breath seized in his throat. "Son of a bitch, you are a pocket Goddess come to life. I want to worship at your feet."

His words brought a smile to her face. Yeah, he was totally screwed. When this job was done, there was no way he was letting her go.

"You're pretty fabulous yourself." Her fingers moved over his chest.

He jerked the ends of his dress shirt out of his slacks, then shrugged the half unbuttoned top off, tossing it to the ground. With her in the heels, bra and panties, he took a step back. Keeping his eyes on her face, his fingers went to work on the belt at his waist then the snap and zipper. Once he was down to the boxer briefs he preferred, he moved back toward her.

"Last chance," he let her feel how hard he was for her. His dick barely contained inside the tight briefs. There was no way in hell he could or would be able to hide his erection.

Those nimble fingers of hers went unerringly down the front of his chest, making him shiver in anticipation, then she stroked him through the thin cloth. "If you ask one more time, I may just have to hurt you." She gave a small squeeze.

"Thank god. Your hand is like poetry in motion." He used his own to release the catch on her bra, loving the little berry tipped mounds.

"Fucking perfect." He bent and took the tip of one into his mouth. Her breath caught, a small mewl accompanied her hand holding his head in place.

He switched to the other nipple, tweaking the one he'd just sucked on between his fingers. Mike wasn't sure what he loved more, hearing the sounds she made, feeling her shiver, or the way she tasted beneath his tongue. He decided it was all the above, but needed more.

Lifting her up, he placed her in the middle of the already turned down bed, then climbed over her, keeping his weight balanced on his forearms as he stared down into her emerald eyes. He could feel her wetness and heat through the thin barrier of her panties. The need for more and the urge to taste all of her, overwhelmed him.

"Mike," she whispered, uncertainty in her voice.

"I'm here. Trying to decide what to do first. You're like all my Christmas wishes come true at once." And she was. His dick jerked telling him exactly where it wanted him to go, but he had other plans, another heated kiss before he moved on to see if her neck was an erogenous zone. Before the night was over, he planned to know everything about Shayna's body. She arched up into him as he licked and sucked his way down her neck into her shoulder, placing tiny biting kisses. When he reached her sensitive breasts, she was panting and writhing beneath him. His woman definitely loved having her nipples sucked and bit. A little pain had her arching against him for more.

"Mike, that feels...oh god, I don't know, but I like it."

He assumed she hadn't much experience, but needed to know how much. His head lifted from her belly. "Tell me if I do anything you don't like, Sile." His hands worked the last bit of covering from her body.

Her fingers ran through his hair. "So far the only thing I don't like is when you stop."

Her words made him laugh. She may be the perfect woman for him. No, scratch that, she was the perfect woman for him. He wedged his shoulders between her thighs, pushing them farther apart.

"Good, I have no plans of stopping." His voice had taken on a sandpaper quality.

His own callused hands parted her folds, the saturated lips of her sex were sweeter looking than anything he'd ever seen. "Has anyone ever eaten this sweet pussy before, Shayna?" he questioned, his lips surrounding her clit, drawing it into his mouth.

Her hands released his hair, shudders shook her and her hands slapped against the bed. He looked up in time to see her fingers tugging at her nipples, harder than he'd have thought.

He drew on the tiny bundle of nerves, then used his tongue, lapping up the slick moisture coating the swollen folds of her sex. Using two fingers, he rimmed her entrance, licking at her with hungry stokes, focusing on her reactions. Using short strokes he teased her, dipping into her vagina while he used his hands to cup her buttocks and lifted her up, giving him better access. "Tell me, Sile," he demanded.

Why he needed, wanted to know, Mike wasn't sure, but the thought of any other man touching her, giving her pleasure ate at him.

His growled words vibrating against her turned her on, if the sweet cream flowing from her pussy like nectar was any indication. He licked it up even as it spilled out of her, his cock aching between his thighs, swelling painfully from the need to sink into her heat.

"More, Mike. I need more," she cried out against his tongue.

"Answer me and I'll give you more than you need, baby."

She arched up, her hips lifting against his face.

"No. Nobody has ever…please fuck me, Mike."

He didn't give her a moment to rethink her words, lifting her higher, he pushed his tongue inside her pussy, making her cry out. Christ, she was tight, clenching on his tongue as he thrust it in and out. Her juices flowing down his chin. He replaced his tongue with two fingers, flicking his tongue over her sensitive clit, lashing it back and forth, moaning as she began clenching down on him. He could feel the throb against his tongue and knew she was ready to come. Surrounding the bundle of flesh, he drew it into his mouth, and added a third finger alongside the other two, and then she was coming apart for him.

Perspiration coated them while she arched against his rapid thrusting fingers into her pussy. His own body was humping the bed. He was more than ready to claim her, but wanted to wait until she was screaming his name.

"Mike, oh yes, right there. Don't stop. Never stop." Her hips rose faster, fucking his face and fingers, and then he felt her pussy ripple around his fingers, the little clit throbbed in his mouth. A second later, she screamed out his name, the sweetest sound he'd ever heard. He couldn't get his boxer briefs off fast enough.

Mike pulled his fingers out, releasing the bundle of nerves from his suctioning mouth with a small kiss and leaned over to the side of the bed, grabbing a condom. The fingers of one hand smoothed the rubber on, while the other gripped the base, rubbing the head in her juices.

"Shayna, look at me," he growled, his lust making it hard to hold back the need but he didn't want to hurt her. "One last time. Are you certain?"

She locked her legs around his thighs. "You really are too honorable. Please, make love to me."

"Once I bury my dick in you, there will be no going back." He had to warn her. She may not realize it, but he was claiming her for more than just this mission. When they caught whoever was after her, Mike planned to still be waking up with Shayna next to him.

Her slick juices coated him, making him want to sink into her.

She lifted her hips, inviting him in with more than just words. He slipped just the head in, the brutal pleasure of being inside Shayna rocked him.

Shit, he had to count to ten to get his bearings, or feared blowing his load. "Damn, you feel so good."

He pushed in a little more, then rocked back out. Repeating the motion until he was all the way inside. Surrounded by her slick heat, he could understand where the poets created the sappy words. If he could, he'd pen one himself.

More of her slick moisture coated him, making it easier for him to move, each thrust shot fiery sensation straight to his balls. Such extreme pleasure, he feared he would come before he got her off. Mike was not a man who ever allowed himself to blow his load before his woman.

Resting on his forearms, he looked at her, then bent and nipped her ear. "You're so tight, you're killing me, Shayna."

He stroked out, then in. Knowing she enjoyed a bit of pain, he levered himself up, and took the tip of one breast into his mouth suckling, then bit down. The ripple along his shaft made his own cock jerk.

"Mike...do that again." She gave a strangled groan.

****

Shayna couldn't believe the things he was making her body feel. He was huge inside her, but her body adjusted to accommodate him. The two lovers she'd had were clearly not in his league. All thoughts of anyone but him flew out the window as he bit down on her flesh again. Her body shook from pleasure-pain. Being stretched almost to the point of pain around him, she couldn't tell where he ended and she began. Each time he pulled out, then thrust back in, she held her breath, knowing the sensation would only get better. He was hitting a spot deep inside her, whipping her body back into a frenzy, a body she was sure couldn't feel such emotions until now.

"Oh, yeah, there you go. Let me feel you come again. Squeeze my cock like you did my fingers, Shayna, let me feel you milk me for all I'm worth," he groaned, pushing into her faster, harder.

The sound of their flesh smacking against each other was all she could hear. His voice whispering dark, erotic words echoed in her ears, an added element that heightened her pleasure, whipping up a storm in her that was new and exciting. Everything with Mike was different, better. The thought of what her life would be like after him almost caused her to seize, but then his pounding strokes hit her bundle of nerves, and all she knew was sensation. Her inner flesh gripped him, one powerful thrust after another. She could feel his cockhead each time he almost slipped out, her body lifting to keep him in her.

And Mike knew it, was willing to give it to her. He didn't hold back, his groans mixed with hers, making it easier to let go.

"That's it, let go. I've got you." He mumbled against her breast then bit down one more time before going up on his knees, speeding up his thrusts. "Come for me, Shayna," he ordered, moving his fingers to her clit.

The orgasm, just out of reach, finally exploded, white-hot in its intensity, making her jerk up, hips lifting taking him deeper. He thrust harder, faster, a lash of fiery pleasure echoed through her entire body as she heard his groan, making shudders wrack her.

"Mike," she screamed as she felt his cock swell inside.

He groaned, hips moving faster, his hands holding her open while he raced toward his own release. In that moment, Shayna was sure her Nana had said she'd one day find her Anam Cara or soulmate as the Irish called it. Only, he was being paid to save her. The irony wasn't lost on her.

She could barely hold her legs up as he released them to slide to the side of the bed. He gave her a hard kiss, then got up. Without the strength to pull the blankets up to cover herself, she lay there waiting for him to return. Even now, after having just been made love to, she could feel her body wanting his. She needed to get a grip. Come morning, he would probably pretend as if nothing had happened, or maybe they'd continue the affair until the danger was over for her.

Rolling to her side took effort, but she didn't want him to see the hurt she knew he'd see at the thought of losing him, before she'd had him.

The bed dipped behind her, then Mike was pulling her to him, tugging the blanket over them both. Silly woman she was, she automatically snuggled into him. She'd deal with whatever was thrown at her when it came. Another thing her Nana always said was don't borrow trouble. Lord, she missed the older woman. When the dust settled, she would make a trip to visit her. The fact her life was one big complication didn't mean she couldn't use a hug from the woman who gave the best advice. Rolling over to face him, she sighed against Mike.

"That sounded like you were thinking a lot. Did I not wear you out enough?" He ran his palm down her back, stopping above her ass.

She shivered, need pooling in her belly. "Oh, I don't know. I could probably be convinced to stay awake." Her own hand wandered down his body. She took her time learning his shape like he'd done her earlier. Keeping up with Mike would definitely take more than she was used to, but Shayna was more than prepared to do it.

The feel of his large hands clenching against her made her bolder. Her sensitive nipples brushed along his side as she moved over him.

"What're you doing, Shayna?"

Tearing her lips from his flesh, she winked. "If you have to ask, I must not be doing it right."

Her fingers stroked down his sides as she ran her lips along the column of his throat, and down his chest, moving slowly down. She longed to taste him, wanted to feel his hard flesh in her mouth and hear him groan in ecstasy.

"Have at it, baby," he said in a low tone, his muscles flexed beneath her. "Be easy, my patience is barely leashed."

"I have faith you'll be able to control yourself," she whispered against him, sitting back on her calves. Looking down at his cock, she was amazed at the size of him. Her tongue peeked out, licking her lips, then she slid it over the wide crest, taking in the bead of precome, loving the subtle salty flavor that was all male.

He jerked. "Shayna love." His words came out strangled, intense, the deep tone almost like gravel that sent a flush of warmth and power through her feminine core. She took him into her mouth, and his hands slid into her hair, guiding her in the rhythm he wanted.

With one hand, she held him at the base, the other she worked him up and down in counterpoint to her mouth. The heavy vein on the underside pounded beneath her tongue, and she could feel his thighs tensing. Mike's guttural, harsh sounds were music to her ears, making her slow, firm caresses increase.

"Shayna, stop. I'm going to come," he warned.

She tightened her mouth around him, and felt his hips rise faster, bucking up. His hands fisted in her hair, the head of his cock pulsed, a strangled groan above her let her know he was about to come. His balls drew up, tension made him hold her tighter, a wildness filled the air, making her feel powerful.

"Damn, Shayna, gonna come." He held her hair back enough so he could see her face, and drove up, fucking her mouth faster, driving into her with wild abandon before he stilled.

She sucked him, drawing his essence into her, swirling her tongue along the ridge beneath the head, licking, lashing the sensitive area, making him shake beneath her. Hearing his breath catch made her smile against his softening cock.

The crazy need to do something she'd never done was something she didn't want to exam too closely.

"I love your mouth, Shayna. Everything about you is perfect." He pulled her next to him, claiming her lips.

Heat flared in the green gaze that caught hers, his expression held something she didn't or couldn't put a name to.

"Hmm, I think you got that wrong, Mr. Royce. You are the one that is perfect and sweet." She ran her hand over his eight pack. Seriously, the man had an eight pack.

"Sweet," he growled.

She nodded. "Most definitely sweet," she promised.

His fingers slid between her thighs, unerringly finding her clit, then moving down, finding her wet. Two thick fingers easily slid into her, her moisture coated them, making his entry easy. "Watch me." He brought the two digits out, coated in her cream and painted her nipple with them. Then, before she knew what he was going to do, he caught the hard bud between his teeth and licked the sheen of her juices from it.

"See, you're the sweet one. You have the tastiest, sweetest pussy I've ever had the pleasure of eating. I could make a meal of you." His rough voice floated over her as his lips moved from one tight peak to the next. "Damn, look how sexy you are. These nipples are so pretty, they get so hard and red when I do this." He bit down on one, then sucked the sting away, moving to do the next, drawing on it with hard pulls of his mouth.

She had to force her eyes open as flashes of electricity tore at her from the top of her head to her toes. Mike gave her no quarter. His hand stroked over the curve of her breasts, down to the juncture between her thighs. She held his gaze even though it was hard to do. His heavy lidded, desire ridden stare held hers, making the intimacy of the act more, holding her a willing prisoner by his power alone. His features turned savage as he stroked through her folds, pressing into her. Her pleasure was his. He took her nipple between his lips again, lashing it with his tongue. The instant jolt of pleasure had her gasping for air. Mike kept on tormenting her flesh, sucking the hardened peak into his mouth, then moving to its twin while stroking in and out of her with his fingers.

Each movement of his body, whether it was his mouth or his fingers, had her need increasing. Juices flowed from her, coating her thighs and his hand.

Desperation had her close to coming, but she didn't want to without him inside her. She wanted to experience that euphoric feeling while his body possessed hers. The chaotic storm was beginning to sweep through her, and she knew she'd be lost if she didn't stop him.

"Mike, I want you inside me when I come again." Her hand moved over his as his finger slid over her clit.

"Let me make you feel good, Shayna." His lips lifted from her.

"You do. Everything about you is wonderful." She fisted her fingers into the sheets at her sides. "Please don't make me wait." She couldn't breathe as he moved down her body, cool air wafted over her, then was replaced by his warm breath. The feel of his tongue running through her folds made her lift up toward him. The sudden need to feel him licking her, circling her clit again, overwhelmed her.

A rumbling growl had her jerking. Tension strained her body like a bow string. She didn't hear the helpless pleas, or the ragged gasps that fell from her mouth with the need whipping through her.

Forcing her fingers to unclench from the bedding, Shayna reached for him, panting. "Please, Mike."

With one last final lick, he lifted his head with a smile, pressing kisses along her frame as he went until he settled over her. He kissed her on the lips, and she tasted herself on him. A hot, toe curling kiss she would forever crave.

Before he placed the broad head of his cock inside of her, he made sure to protect her, always ensuring her safety. The crisp hair on his thighs pushed hers apart, spreading her, rubbing her swollen folds and then pressing forward. They moaned in unison as he entered her.

"Heaven," he swore. "Being inside you is as close to heaven as I'll ever be on Earth." Then he began to move. Bending, he took her lips in a deep, tongue thrusting kiss.

Each time he touched her it was the most pleasure she'd ever felt. Then he would move, and she would swear it was the best. Each stroke, each kiss, each caress, better than the last until she was being thrown into a kaleidoscope of ecstasy, deeper into pleasure so intense it bordered on pain. Her hips raised to meet his, moving frantically, racing toward what Mike could give her. What she feared only he could give her.

"Yes, yes, oh my god, yes." She held him to her. The sensations lashing at her strongly. Her nails bit into him but he didn't seem to care, or notice. Damp with perspiration, their slick bodies made slapping sounds that echoed in the room, but nothing mattered to them but each other.

Until finally, the explosion came. Her back arched, legs squeezing his hips and she swore her heart shattered along with her body. His shout and hers mingled, and then he was collapsing over her, still keeping most of his weight off of her.

A part of her wished he would stay where he was, but then he slipped out and off, rolling to his feet to take care of the spent condom. When he returned, he pulled her against him and she let sleep take her, secure in his arms.

Chapter Seven

Shayna woke, pleasantly sore in all the right places. Throughout the night, she'd known Mike held her. Before someone had targeted her after taking the violin, she wasn't aware of the danger, but now that she was under Mike's protection, she wasn't able to forget. Her job was to play the violin for money, but she had more than enough to never have to do so again. She thought of what she could do with her talent, and she came to the conclusion that traveling all around the world didn't appeal. But, where did that leave her with Mike Royce was the biggest question.

"Good morning, beautiful." Mike's deep rumble had her looking up.

Early morning sunlight barely filtered into the windows, casting shadows over them. "Morning." She felt shy and the need to use the restroom, had her moving away from his warm body. "I need to use the bathroom." Mortified at her words, she tried to roll away.

"Hey, don't pull away from me." He held her against him. "Go do what you have to do, then we'll talk."

She nodded, then hopped out of the bed. After using the facilities, she stared at herself in the mirror, looking to see if she appeared different. Surely, after the night of pleasure she'd had in Mike's arms, any woman would. Slight red marks marred her neck and breasts, and the inner parts of her thighs. Instead of heading straight back out, a quick shower was in order.

By the time she walked back out to the bedroom, Mike was gone. She wasn't aware she was hoping to see him until he wasn't there. Another new dress was lying on the perfectly made bed, making her realize her quick retreat hadn't been all that quick. Well, a woman could be forgiven for taking the time to look presentable. It wasn't like she often slept with a man she'd only just met, but something was different with this one.

With Mike Royce, she felt a deeper connection, and she knew it was dangerous. He was there to protect her, not fall in love with her. Shayna's mind came to a stuttering halt.

"Oh my God, I can't love him," she whispered to the empty room. However, her heart knew different. Just like all the other females in her family, she'd fallen fast and hard. It was said that the women in her family, who were all crazy Irish as her father called them, would know their soul mates. They'd find the one meant for them, even when they weren't looking. Her father said it didn't matter, because somehow their hearts would know, and they'd fall head-over-ass in love.

She shut her eyes and willed the feelings to the back of her mind, but her heart still beat just as fast. "Damn you, Irish blood."

"You talk to yourself a lot?" Mike stood in the doorway, his amused tone too sexy for words.

Shayna took a deep breath and then let it out before answering. "Only when I need to give myself a talking to, aye."

He nodded, then stepped further into the room. "I called the boutique we visited and had them send up another dress yesterday. I hope you don't mind."

She had forgotten she was standing in nothing but a towel. Luckily she was pretty confident in her appearance, but the heated look he was giving her told her he planned to wreck the time she'd spent in the bathroom. A fact her body was completely on board with.

Mike stopped an arm's length from her. "Shit," he growled, pulling out his cell. "Royce here, this better be good."

Listening to his one-sided conversation, the relaxed man was replaced by the protector who was hired on by the Alpha Team. When he slid the small device back into his pocket, she met his green eyes. "What happened?"

"That was Greg. They found a lead on who stole the Stradivarius, but didn't want to go into details. They want us to come back to the office." He looked at his watch.

She knew exactly what he was thinking. Her body wanted the same thing. His in hers. Her stomach growled, making her embarrassed.

"Come on, I ordered room service. We can eat after you get dressed. If you continue to flaunt that gorgeous body, I can't promise we'll make it back up to Tampa before tomorrow." He raised his hand, running the pads of his fingers over the swell of her breasts. The heat of his words and the touch of his hands let her know he was telling the truth.

It took her a few seconds to get her tongue unstuck from the roof of her mouth. "Okay," she agreed.

Mike licked his bottom lip. "Fuck it, I need a taste." Then he bent and took her lips in a kiss that bordered on frantic.

Her knees threatened to buckle. When he lifted his head, she knew her legs were shaking, and her breathing was choppy. With his chest rising and falling as hard as hers, she knew he was as affected as her, making her feel like she wasn't a total idiot. "You better leave so I can get dressed, otherwise I won't be responsible for attacking you." Truer words had never been spoken.

His head jerked up and down once then he took a step back, spun around and walked out of the room, taking all the oxygen with him.

Her ass hit the bed. "The man is potent like the finest wine," she swore staring at the empty doorway.

Looking at the gorgeous white dress she shook her head. The man did have exquisite taste, though. She quickly put on the dress he'd purchased, barely stopping herself from blushing as she thought about the lingerie he'd bought her to go with it.

Mike stood by a table with a few covered dishes as she entered the dining area of the suite. The scent of bacon and eggs had her hurrying across the floor. "It smells delicious. What did you order?" She sank gratefully into the chair he held out.

"A little of everything I think." His teasing tone sent a shiver down her spine. Or maybe it was the way he said it, while he pressed an open mouthed kiss to her neck before he took a seat across from her.

They finished eating, and then it was time to head back. A sense of foreboding hit Shayna.

"Hey, I'll keep you safe." Mike reached for her.

Shayna felt silly, knowing he'd do exactly as he said. Hell, the thief had no reason to come after her. They had the multi-million dollar violin. They had no reason to come for her.

After ensuring the hallway was clear, he led her out of the suite. He tugged on her hand, pulling her to a stop. "Do you trust me?" He asked.

Nodding, she squeezed his hand and stayed as close to him as possible until they got into the vehicle, not realizing she had been holding her breath most of the time.

"I was a wee bit worried you were going to pass out on me a few times back there," Mike said as he eased his sports car into the Miami traffic. Like everything else he did, he maneuvered through it all with precision and confidence. The only thing

Shayna felt she did anything so well in, was instruments.

Taking a deep breath, she let it out. Miles of highway stretched out before them. They made a stop halfway between. Mike grabbed her arm. "Wait for me," he reminded her as she went to get out.

She looked around the truck stop, which looked almost deserted. "You don't think whoever took the violin is following us?" she asked looking over her shoulder.

He gave a slight squeeze. "It's better to be safe than sorry."

****

The back of his neck itched. Never a good thing in his line of work. He'd keep driving, but they needed fuel and he'd seen the way she was bouncing in the seat. Mike knew when a lady needed to go to the restroom. He chose a truck stop that he'd seen on their way down. One he was sure he could get in and out of easily, and also was close to the highway. Reassuring Shayna he could keep her safe from a thief was the easy part, saving her from him was going to be the hard part. He was not a man made for the happily forever kind like some of his friends. Not like his partner. No, he had too much baggage. Hell, he was known for killing first and asking questions later. Maddox even joked he had too many body counts on his record, but what his partner didn't know was Mike had even more that he didn't know about.

Not wanting the past to creep into his present, he got out of the car and filled the tank before striding around the front to help Shayna out. She was all lightness to his dark. Too good for him. If she knew about his past and how he'd let the last woman who loved him, along with her unborn child die, would she still look at him the way she had in that hotel suite? He knew the answer to that question. A resounding Hell no. Of course, everyone said it wasn't his fault. He'd fallen hard and fast for a woman who he thought was one thing, but she'd been something else entirely. A snort escaped his tight control.

"You okay?" Shayna blinked up at him, bringing him back to the present.

He stared down at her, realizing he was standing with her out in the middle of the open area unprotected. "Yeah, sorry. Was thinking."

She patted his chest. "Well, if it hurts that much, stop it."

Her bright smile brought a grin to his lips. "Come on smarty pants." He took her elbow and led her into the store past the cashier. A young girl too engrossed in a magazine than them.

He stopped outside the ladies room. "Since it's a single stall I want you to go in and lock the door. Don't come out until I knock and let you know I'm out here. Got it?" He kept a firm grip on her arm, needing her to know he meant business.

With a nod, she gave a slight tug. "I got it."

Listening until he heard the lock engage, he went across the hall to the men's room and quickly used the facilities. The memory of the last woman he'd allowed himself to care about flashed before his eyes. She'd been the polar opposite of Shayna, blonde and blue eyed. Tall and willowy. Unbeknownst to him, she'd been an operative pretending to be an airheaded model. Hell, he should've known better, but he'd been blown away by her beauty. Not that he couldn't attract beautiful women, but she'd been young and had pursued him. He'd not been one to follow fashion, but while he'd been in Paris on a mission, he had seen her on billboards. What operative would flash their face across anything so large he'd thought at the time? For months they'd dated, and he'd taken her to many different countries with her blowing off contracts with other modeling agencies. Or so he'd thought. Never had he taken her without protection. He'd never taken any woman without protection.

The man staring back at him was the same one he'd seen every day for the past thirty-five years.

The same dark hair and green eyes. On more than one occasion he'd been told he could be Jason Momoa's twin, except his green eyes. On the day he'd been confronted with Daviana and her duplicity, his world was rocked.

"What the hell is going on?" Mike stared at the scene before him, although it was pretty clear what was going on. Daviana, the woman he'd been sure was in love with him. The woman who he'd been sleeping with for the past few months, was in bed with a man. A man he knew was a criminal.

Daviana pulled the sheet over her naked body. "Royce, what are you doing back so early? I thought you would be gone until tomorrow?" Cold calculation stared back at him from her cornflower blue eyes.

His back straightened. The man next to her kept his eyes on Mike, but he didn't make a move. "My trip didn't take as long as I'd thought. I had planned to surprise you. Surprise," he said without a hint of humor. His eyes tracked them both. Not once did his lover show an ounce of fear, or regret.

"Why don't you go in the other room while we get dressed so we can talk like civilized adults." Daviana made it sound like a demand coated in sugar.

He'd always thought her accent was sexy as fuck, but now it grated. "I have seen everything beneath the sheets, darling, so why don't you both ease on out of there and get dressed where I can see you both." His hand went to the gun he had in the back of his pants. In that brief second, he realized she truly had feelings for the man in the bed. Raul was a killer who cared for no one.

"Please, Mike," she begged.

Taking his eyes off of the threat, he saw tears swimming in her eyes. A huge mistake he regretted instantly as Raul rolled out of the bed and began firing at him. Mike returned fire, but his fear for Daviana, even though she was not his woman kept his attention splintered.

He felt the sting of a bullet graze his arm, but he made it into the living area, assessing the best place to defend himself and worried for Daviana. "Fuck a duck."

Raul emerged with Daviana in a man's T-shirt, his arm banded about her throat. "I suggest you come on out, or I'll kill the woman."

Mike knew it wasn't a threat, but he was on a mission. One that meant he had to choose. He looked around the corner, and could see the woman who he'd thought cared for him held against the man she'd clearly been screwing just moments before. Both individuals looked way too comfortable in the position they were in to be amateurs at the game. Mike wondered how many other men had fallen for the same trick as he had.

"I think I'll just stay where I am until the rest of my team get here, Raul." He let them both know he was onto them, watching to see how his words affected them both.

A gasp left Daviana's mouth, while Raul showed no emotion.

"I'm sorry to hear that, Royce. You know it has been fun, but...well, it is survival of the fittest."

Raul pressed a kiss to his lovers' cheek moments before he shoved her from him.

"What the hell, Raul?" she questioned him.

The operative held his gun up, pointing straight at her head. "Sorry, love, but I can't be taken in."

Daviana placed her hand over her throat, her other one over her stomach. Mike watched her head swing between where he was hiding and to Raul. "I'm pregnant."

Bile swam into his stomach, but he knew it couldn't be his. Hell, it could be. Condoms weren't a hundred percent. Fuck!

"You said you were protected," Raul accused.

A shiver shook her frame. "I had to have the inner uterine device taken out last month, but the doctor said I should still be fine."

Raul laughed harshly. "Well, then I guess it's a good thing I am about to do this then."

Before Mike could stop him, Raul fired off two killing shots. One between Daviana's eyes, and the other her heart. Not stopping to think, he aimed and *shot Raul in the exact same areas, forgetting they needed the man alive. Forgetting the CIA wanted information from the bastard who'd just killed a woman who was possibly carrying his child.*

Mike came back to the present at the sound of someone banging on the door. Shit! He quickly washed and dried his hands. He'd been lost in the past and a nightmare that had nearly unmanned him. He'd hoped like hell Daviana was lying about being pregnant, but when the autopsy had come back, his world nearly crumbled. Had he handled the entire situation differently, she may have lived to become a mother. Her child could be alive today. Hell, he had to quit thinking about that fateful day and concentrate on saving Shayna from some crazed stalker.

He knocked on the women's bathroom door and waited. When she didn't open or say anything after a couple minutes, he tried the door, shocked to find it unlocked. Easing the door open he swept inside to find it empty.

He went to the front of the store, taking a quick look around, then came back to the young clerk. "Did you see a woman leave here?"

The girl lay the magazine down and gave him her attention. "Um, yeah. I mean, there was a man and woman who left a few minutes ago."

Mike tossed a hundred dollar bill on the counter. "Did you see which way they went?"

She looked at the money, then at him. "He was pretty scary looking." She picked up the money before continuing. "I think they headed north in a black SUV."

"Thank you," he said tossing another large bill down.

"Is she your girlfriend?" She bit her pierced lip.

Without giving himself too much time to think about what he was saying, he nodded. "She's my everything."

"Go get her then. I thought she looked scared, but then again, I wasn't paying too much attention."

The young girl looked sheepish, but he didn't have time to chat. He raised his hand in farewell, and was out the door. Inside his vehicle, he pulled up the GPS tracker he'd placed on Shayna without her knowledge. He'd sewn the small device into the hem of the dress while she'd been showering as a precaution. Now he was glad his overprotective instincts were in full swing. While he drove, the monitor pulled up her location, and sure as shit, the beacon lit up, showing they were heading North. His breath whooshed out of him.

"Call Greg Holmes," he ordered the wireless cell.

Ringing echoed through the car. "Holmes here, this better be good."

"Shayna's been taken. I've got a tracker on her, but wanted to give you an update. Do you have anything new for me about the person who took the violin?" He wouldn't normally admit to anything until he had fixed a fuckup, but with Shayna he'd do anything to ensure her safety.

"We've located the violin, but not the buyer, or the thief. Tay and Jaqui are doing some digging for me as well. I will have answers." Greg's tone held no inflection.

The very fact he'd called in some favors from two members of SEAL Team Phantom gave him a bit of hope. "Keep me posted if you find anything else. I'll update you after I get Shayna back."

"Kai's sending in one of his guys who happens to be down there on vacation. I've given him your location and from my calculations, he's parallel to you, don't ask me how," Greg muttered.

Mike didn't say he could give two shits about who was or wasn't near him unless they could get to Shayna first. After he explained what happened, leaving out his trip down memory lane, he disconnected before Greg could ask more.

His vehicle roared down the highway, sliding between cars. At one point he took the shoulder, uncaring the gravel was tearing up his undercarriage. The sight of the red dot indicating

Shayna was growing closer had his heart racing faster.

"I'm coming for you Sile, hang tough." He gripped the wheel tightly between his fingers.

Up ahead he saw two identical SUVs but only one had his woman inside. Gut churning, he hung back. Worry for her safety ate at him. If he pressed, the kidnapper could kill her without allowing him to negotiate for her release. Or, they could wreck, injuring or killing her in the process. His last option was to wait until they stopped. Waiting wasn't his strong suit.

Another half hour flew by, each second felt like a year, until finally the vehicle he'd been trailing pulled off the highway. Mike stayed back farther than he liked. The small airstrip in the middle of nowhere left him no choice. He couldn't allow the other vehicle with Shayna inside to get close enough, yet as they neared, another vehicle sat waiting.

"Fuck a duck," he muttered.

He reached into the backseat without taking his eyes off the road and located the weapons bag he always kept handy. Setting it in the passenger seat he made sure it was open. It may not be an ideal situation, nor the best place to die, but he'd go down in a blaze of bullets before he'd allow Shayna to think he hadn't done his best to save her.

His foot hit the gas, roaring in front of the SUV. The startled look of the driver along with the fear in Shayna's eyes had resolve racing along his veins. His sweet little ride was more than a fast car. It was equipped with monocoque, the principal component of the car's chassis. The monocoque includes the driver's survival cell and cockpit, which was surrounded by 'deformable crash-protection structures' that absorb energy during a crash, plus a 6mm layer of carbon and Zylon which was used in armored vests. He'd had the car specially constructed so things like carbon fiber splinters wouldn't injure the driver in the event of a crash, very similar to NASCAR drivers' cars. He spun the wheel until he faced the SUV, and waited, expecting the man driving to stop, but prepared to be rammed. In his sporty car, he knew the big vehicle would appear to be the threat, lending the other driver a sense of confidence.

Through the windshield he saw cold calculation enter the man behind the wheel's eyes. Moments before impact, Mike pressed down on the gas, and turned, aiming for the wheels. The front two tires flattened as his own car took a slight hit on the back end. He spun the car around again, this time he was the one with the upper hand. The plane on the tarmac fired up, the car and its occupants raced away, only to be stopped by several vehicles pouring in. Mike recognized the Alpha Team leader, but his focus was centered on Shayna. The black vehicle kept moving forward, the flat tires slowing it down.

Having no other option, he accelerated, aiming for the front of the vehicle. The impact was jarring to both of them, the airbags filled the interior of the SUV, making the other vehicle swerve then come to a stop. Mike jerked the handle of his car door open, hopped out and rounded the wreckage with a singular intent. He had his gun in one hand, going to Shayna's door first. The locked handle pissed him off, but he kept his cool. The airbag on her side had exploded, but he could see her trying to push it aside, then watched as she noticed he was there.

"Open the door," he ordered.

She did as he instructed, then he was holding her in his arms, something he feared he'd never get to do again. Her trembling had him wanting to hold her in the most primitive way, but they were far from out of danger.

"Come on. I need you to get in the car, and stay there." Mike made sure he kept her behind him, listening for the other occupants.

Shayna didn't protest. A fact he'd reward her for later, he mentally swore.

Once he had her safely inside his car, he went back to check on the driver, finding the man gone. Pulse racing, he inched around the hood. A man stood with his arm raised, the gun was leveled and then a shot rang out.

Mike rolled, barely missed being shot, coming back up and taking his aim, firing where he'd seen the shooter. A grunt, and thud followed. Not willing to make another mistake, he inched over, finding the man lying on the dirt with a gunshot wound to his shoulder and a contusion to his forehead. Mike kicked the gun that had fallen from the kidnapper away before he flipped the man onto his stomach. Using zip ties he always carried to restrain him, he didn't allow himself to relax.

"Release me, asshole, and I'll tell you whatever you want to know." The Russian accent gave him a slight pause.

Mike rolled him back over, knowing it was causing the man more pain. "Who hired you?"

The Russian spit dirt out of his mouth. "I will only speak if you promise me amnesty."

Hearing him say such words shouldn't have shocked Mike, but they did.

Movement off to his left, had him spinning, gun up and ready.

"Ah, now, I don't think that is necessary, my friend."

A tall willowy man in his late forties stood with another man flanking him. The one who spoke looked almost feminine aside from his prominent Adams apple and deep voice. He also had a Russian accent, only his was more polished.

Mike was no dummy. The real threat was the man behind the sophisticated one. The brute of a man had to be close to six and a half feet tall and weighed more than Mike did, which was saying a lot since Mike weighed in at two hundred and fifty pounds at last count.

"I don't believe we're friends," Mike said in a cold voice.

The man who'd spoke tilted his head. "Well now, that's a shame. I would've preferred to have been friendly, than...not." He lifted a pale hand, then stepped aside.

The giant stepped forward. Mike took aim, and shot the big bastard in his right kneecap. Fuck being civilized. It was one of the reasons he was known as the killer. He didn't play nice, and he sure as shit didn't stand around and shake his dick in a measuring contest.

"What the bloody hell?" Pale guy asked. "Are you crazy?"

He nodded. "Does a bear shit in the woods?" Mike looked at the big guy rolling around on the ground. Pussy. Shoot a man in the knee and they get all crybaby like.

The man Mike had begun to call Pale guy took a step back, then shook his arms out. "What does that even mean? Of course bears shit in the woods."

He shrugged. "It doesn't matter, now, turn around," his words were cut off as the man tossed a knife with precision at him. The move was so unexpected, Mike barely had a second to realize what was happening. The pain sent him to the ground, dropping his gun, which was clearly the man's intent.

"Tsk, tsk. You should never judge a book by its cover, Mr. Royce." Polished black boots came into his line of sight.

His right arm hung limply from the knife imbedded in it. "And you should never wear those shoes. They don't go with that belt. Don't you watch Fashion Police?" Mike gritted out.

"What is this you speak of? These are Armani." The toe of the shoe in question lifted as if the man was checking them out.

Mike ripped the knife out of his shoulder. The searing pain was pushed back as he used the distraction of clothing choices. He stabbed down with the point of the blade through the expensive leather. The squeal had him smiling for only a moment, before a swift kick to his injured shoulder had him dropping the weapon and rolling away. He came back up onto his feet, his mind already calculating his next move.

"Armani, Sharmani. They are ugly as fuck, just the same as you. What the heck are you into? Twilight or what? Don't you watch the news? Edward is out this year. Sparkly vampires are no longer the in thing." Mike shook his head and pretended to be sad for the man's ignorance. He could tell this man truly took his appearance as the utmost importance. Although he'd clearly underestimated him once, he wouldn't again.

Limping slightly, the pale man moved forward. "You don't know who you are messing with. I am richer than Midas. I pay to have only the best of everything. I can buy and sell you ten times over. Just like that." He snapped his fingers.

His words were beginning to make a bit of sense to Mike. This man had seen Shayna, and like a child, he wanted her. More than likely she wasn't the first woman he'd decided to collect. The thought sickened him. "So you do what? Steal them and keep them until you get tired of playing your sick games? Sort of like a spoiled little boy. Sorry to burst your bubble, little man, but you picked the wrong lady this time."

Hate burned in the man's eyes. "I am not little."

Mike couldn't believe the expertise with which the other man began to fight. He dodged the flying kick, grunting in pain as several punches landed on his injured shoulder and unprotected side. Finally, he pushed the pain to the back of his mind. Knowing his right arm was completely out of commission, he employed his martial arts training, focusing on his legs.

With a spinning kick, he knocked the man to the ground, then fell on top of him, hitting him unmercifully with his one good arm until he no longer fought back. He pictured Shayna at the hands of this man until he was through with her. Her beautiful face no longer lit with laughter. "Never," he roared.

The sound of grunts near him began to penetrate the fog in his mind. The need to ensure the man below him never harmed a hair on Shayna's head lessened as words filtered in through the red haze of hate.

"Mike, you can stop now. I think he's stopped fighting, man." Greg Holmes deep voice penetrated his tunnel vision, yet he needed to ensure Shayna's safety. He couldn't allow her eyes to close. She couldn't end up like the last woman he'd cared about.

"Do you want me to, tackle him or shoot him?"

"Mike, please," Shayna whispered.

He looked up to see the object of his desires standing with tears streaking down her face, then glanced down to see the bloody pulp of a mess he'd made of the monster beneath him. He looked at his one bruised and bloody hand, then at her beautiful face, and once pristine white dress. It took monumental effort for him to climb off of the limp body beneath him. He watched the bastard's chest rise and fall, taking a measure of ease in the fact he hadn't killed the sonofabitch. Standing next to Shayna was a huge red-haired man he recognized. Oz from SEAL Team Phantom, the crazy bastard looked as if he'd just jumped out of a plane.

Turning his back to Shayna, he couldn't stand to see the revulsion in her eyes, he looked at Greg. "Get her out of here." When it didn't appear as though the older man was going to comply, he took a step closer. "Now, Greg. Get her the fuck out of here."

Her whimper tore his heart out. Damn, he didn't want her to see him for the monster he was.

"Take her home, Greg, I got this," Oz said.

He shut out the sound of her whimpers until the only sound he heard was his own harsh breaths.

"Well, that sure is gonna take a lot of money to fix."

Mike looked back at the mess of a man, then up at the crazy SEAL. "He's a sick twisted fuck."

Oz shook his head. "I meant your car. You need to learn how to take care of sweet things like that." He let out a sigh then walked over to the man on the ground. "He's more than a mess, but I'm sure he'll be right as rain in no time."

"How'd you get here so quick?" Mike took a deep inhale of warm air followed by another. Anything to take his mind off the fact he'd just let his heart leave with Greg.

"From the sky." Oz pointed up.

"Say what?" At over six feet three, the other man was big by anyone's standards. With the bright red hair and jovial attitude, most thought he was a good ole country boy. However, Mike knew Oz Couper was one of the deadliest and most skilled members of SEAL Team Phantom. Of course, he was also one of the craziest sons of bitches too.

"You see, I don't like to risk wrecking a perfectly fine piece of machinery like that. Therefore, I figure out the right trajectory and just jump. Most times with a chute, I might add." Oz had pointed at Mike's dented up vehicle while he spoke.

"You just happened to be in a plane, when the call came in, that I needed a little backup?" Even to his own ears that sounded farfetched.

Bright white teeth flashed as Oz began jogging backwards toward what was clearly his parachute lying on the tarmac as men in suits began filling the area. "I'm on vacation. Don't know what you're talking about. I was never here." He winked as a big SUV roared its way toward them, stopping a couple inches away from where Oz stood with his arms full of parachute material. "Well, would you look at the time. I'll just be on my way seeing as how my ride is right on time. You might wanna have that arm seen to."

The mention of his wound had him grimacing. He'd almost forgotten about his own injury, yet nothing could compare to the feeling of losing Shayna. There was no way he could face her and see her look away in disgust after seeing what he'd done.

Chapter Eight

Shayna paced the hotel room floor for what she was sure was the hundredth time. Two damn weeks she'd been in Tampa. Two weeks too long since she'd watched Mike stomp away from her after telling Greg to get her the fuck out of there. Well, she had news for him. She was not leaving without a fight.

After the Alpha Team had swooped in, she had been shocked to learn Dimitri, a Russian diplomat's son had been infatuated with her after watching her play the violin. He'd orchestrated the theft of the violin, knowing that J&A Beare would be compensated, and had planned to return the violin after her death. Of course, he didn't know how long he'd keep her as all his playmates differed. A shiver wracked her frame. The billionaire playboy would have gotten away with his plans had she not gone to Greg and Amelia for help. When officials had searched his homes, they'd found little souvenirs from several women, twelve to be exact. Twelve women who had been missing all over the world, but none had been connected with him, until now.

"He can't get you now," she reassured herself. Two of the women were Americans, making him face the United States justice system.

"You know it's not a good thing to talk to yourself?"

She spun around, heart racing at the sound of the deep voice behind her. Mike Royce, the man she'd been dreaming about, needing, wanting for the past two weeks stood near the balcony doors. After weeks with no word he was looking too damn good for her peace of mind. "What are you doing here?"

He took a step away from the wall. "I couldn't stay away. How do you live without your heart?" he asked. "I can't do it anymore, Shayna."

Her own heart banged against her chest. "I don't know."

"There were days when I would wish to bleed, to feel pain, just to know that I was alive. Now, with you, I finally realized what it is to actually live for the first time. It only took a smile from you, and my heart would race, my dick would harden. Before you, there were times I would go days, weeks or more when the world didn't see me. At times I didn't think anyone would miss me if I was killed, other than Maddox. Now that he's with Hailey, even he would probably forget about me."

She put her arms around him, reached up and covering his mouth with her hand. "Don't say that. You mean so much, to so many people. If you don't believe me, then think again because you do to all of us. These past two weeks, I missed you so much. I missed the way my hand felt in yours. I missed your teasing ways. I missed the way you referred to the Real Housewives, and knowing you really did like them. I've even started watching them. Just to feel closer to you. Please, don't leave me again." A tear fell down her cheek, another one joined the first. His words of needing to bleed, just to know he was alive struck a nerve within her.

His knuckles grazed her cheek, drying her tears. "You're too good for me, but I can't let you go. I tried. Dammit, I tried. I'm just not that good of a man."

Again, she put her hand over his mouth. The feel of his tongue licking her palm made her smile in spite of the situation. "You are a better man than you give yourself credit for. And, before you say another stupid word, let me warn you, I will smack you if you don't let me finish."

He grinned behind her palm. "You're feisty. I like that."

"I know something bad must've happened for you to run from me, but whatever it is, we can work through it. I love you, Mike. I know it's too soon, but there it is. I love you, and you'll just have to deal with it. The men and women in the Macintyre Clan fall hard, and we fall fast, so just let that sink in and deal."

****

He stared in awe at the little vixen telling him she loved him, and that he'd just have to deal. He'd laugh if he wasn't too damn humbled. "I fucking love you, too. The Royce's don't really do anything fast, but we also don't do anything by half measures. I swear to all that I'll love you to the end of time, and then I'll love you beyond that. When we are old and grey, and then dust, I'll still love you." The words weren't just words, they were a promise, ones he'd keep.

"I think I can handle that as long as I have you." He cradled her face in his palms, then unable to stop himself, he captured her lips in a kiss that he hoped conveyed his feelings. All the pent up longings, the suffering he'd gone through while thinking he was doing the right thing flowed out of him. His arm ached from the knife wound, yet the doctors had said there was no nerve or muscle damage. The stitches had come out a few days ago, and he'd debated with himself until he'd finally came to his senses.

"That's good to hear. There are a lot of things you will learn about me, and stubborn is another one." The sheen of tears had made her green eyes sparkle.

Her porcelain fine skin looked too smooth for his rough touch, but he couldn't stop from touching her. "I think I'm up for the challenge."

She looked down to where his dick was most definitely showing its presence. "Hmm, I can see that," she laughed.

Mike grunted. "Ignore him, I have." For the last fourteen days he had done just that. It was the hardest damn two weeks of his life.

"Why don't we go sit down, you look a little better than the last time I saw you, but I need to make sure you're truly okay."

He couldn't believe this woman. "You know, I can't remember the last time someone wanted to make sure I was okay because they worried about me. I mean my bosses did because they had a job for me, but, yeah, I'll shut up now."

He sat on the sofa in the luxurious seating room. A guy might get drunk and spout all kinds of bullshit, but he didn't have an excuse, other than he was drunk on love. He wanted Shayna to understand she was special.

She gave him a slight press into the center of the couch, then bit on her thumb. "I'm gonna have to see your wound." With a nod, she began unbuttoning his top.

He sat while she straddled his lap. "Baby, I don't know if you realize this, but you're torturing me."

Her hands with the calluses on the tips running over his exposed skin, made him shiver. Every inch of flesh she revealed she kissed. Finally, she had his top completely open. "Damn, did I ever tell you I didn't believe an eight pack ab was real?"

Green eyes met his, twinkling with arousal. He liked that she enjoyed his body. He especially liked that she was comfortable enough to straddle him in her flirty little dress. His hands reached up, brushing over her smooth thighs under the skirt. "I'm glad you approve."

"If I was a painter, I'd paint you just like this," she said stroking her fingers across his shoulders, pushing the shirt out of the way.

He helped her until he had his left arm out, then the right. "Too bad I wasn't an artist. I'd take great delight in laying you out just so and painting you naked. I'd use blacks and whites with a bit of green to match your eyes."

He frowned as she didn't say a word. "What's wrong, Sile."

She bent and kissed the healing wound. "I hate that you were injured because of me."

Grabbing the back of her hair, he pulled her head back, making her meet his gaze. "Baby, I'd take a bullet for you. I'd step in front of a dozen knives, a speeding car, whatever, for you. Don't you get that? You are the color to my world. I was seeing in shades of black and grey. The sun came out when I saw you. It may sound corny, but you're my sunshine."

"You know, I can actually play 'You Are My Sunshine' on the violin."

"After hearing you play Metallica, I don't doubt for a minute you could play anything on it." He was finding it hard to form words with her straddling him.

"Are you hurting still?" she asked at his wince.

"I am, yes." He kept his face straight as he said the words.

"Where?"

"Are you going to kiss it all better when I tell you?" He held her by the hips under her dress now, loving the feel of her warm flesh beneath his fingers. Although his right arm was screaming at him, he held it where it was.

She squirmed on his lap, trying to get off of him. "Anything you need." Her words were cut off short as she felt his bulge beneath her. "Oh, and is that where your boo boo is?"

He lifted his hips up, making them both groan. "He really does hurt the most."

Eyes narrowing, she wiggled off of him. "Well, why didn't you say so?"

Mike swore the angels began to sing, or maybe that was not the right thing to think about as Shayna knelt on the rug in between his spread thighs and began undoing his belt, then the snap to his jeans. His breath hissed out of him while she released the zipper. He raised his ass, allowing her to maneuver them down and off. Fuck, he couldn't remember a time when he was buckass naked or almost, while a woman was fully clothed. The vision in front of him was one he'd forever have burned into his brain. Shayna licking her lips, and then leaning forward to lick the head of his cock, taking the bead of milky white fluid into her mouth. She gripped his dick in her palm, running her fist up and down all the way to his balls, harder than he'd thought she would.

"Ah, shit, fuck…" Mike's head fell back against the back of the couch, but his fingers itched to hold her to him.

Her mouth was tight, wet and nearly had him coming like an untried teen boy. Each stroke, each lick, brought him closer to the edge. Tingles of sensation sent erotic fires through him, making his dick harder, and the little minx in front of him knew it. Relished it.

It was a no brainer which choice he'd make. Fuck her face, or make love to her. All he had to do was yank her over his hardened flesh, and thrust inside her, or just let her continue to suck him. Either option was a win win for him. Her tongue licked the glistening tip, her parted lips wet and swollen, and he decided he needed to taste her, even though she was magic however she worked him. His hips jerked in protest, wanting to fill her.

"Come here, love, I want to be inside you. The first time I come again, I want to be buried so deep inside you, we both forget where we end or begin. It'll be us instead of you or me." His fingers bit into her hips as she stood up and shimmied out of her panties.

"You're so damn gorgeous. I'm not worthy, but damn if I'll let you go." The words came out in a rush, but she shushed him with a sweet kiss and climbed onto his lap, lifting the skirt out of the way.

She made a little incoherent word as she sank down on him, the sound made him want to come right then and there. Up and down she moved, taking him higher while their mouths fused together.

He nipped at her lips, then dropped open mouthed kisses along her neck and throat, tugging at the bodice of the dress she wore. She made him feel whole and want the elusive happily ever after.

Cupping her face in his left palm, he kept her eyes glued to his. "Shit, I forgot a condom."

Remembering the latex, or lack of it for the first time in his thirty plus years, he cursed the need for it. He loved feeling her wet warm heat surrounding him.

"Good, I love how you feel inside me. I've never...I mean, this is my first time with anyone without one, and I'm protected," she whispered.

Her words triggered something deep and primal in him. He let out a groan, then stood with her in his arms, nearly falling as his jeans around his hips fell to his ankles. Laughing, he kicked them all the way off along with his shoes and carried Shayna to the bedroom. His dick was still buried deep within her heat.

The bed dipped beneath their weight, and then he realized she had her dress on, something he needed to rectify. "Your dress offends me, woman," he gave a mock growl.

She raised her hips, rolling them in a provocative way. "Well, we must not offend you."

In an economy of motion, Shayna had her dress off and he tossed it away from them. Next, he silenced any other word she might say away, kissing her lips, her nose, her cheeks. Covering her with as much love and affection as he could, then moved his lips to her breast and enclosed it. She mewled and lifted her leg up to his upper thigh, opening herself to him more.

Mike circled her nipple, then bit down on it, making her groan and her pussy clench. Her pleasure was his. The rippling of her inner muscles made her a tighter fit, but Mike knew they were made for each other, and he'd gladly spend the rest of his life saving Shayna. She'd already saved him.

"God I love you, Shayna. I never knew this feeling truly existed until I met you, but I swear, I'll be the best man for you." He slid back and forth slowly, punctuating each word with an inward thrust inside her. "Fuck, I could stay inside you forever."

"I don't think we'd get much done if we did that," she quipped.

He could tell the prospect appealed to her as much as him as her juices made it easier for him to move. He didn't think he'd last much longer. Wanting her to come before he did, rolling to his back, he stared up at her. "I need you to come for me. Milk my cock, baby."

Reaching between their bodies he plied her little clit with his thumb, loving the way her green eyes lit up with passion. She was too sweet, soft, and sexy and Mike lost himself in the hot clasp of her body. Her pussy gripped him tight as he thrust up and rubbed her in tight circles, and then just as he was sure he would leave her behind, he felt her begin to squeeze his cock. He thrust up and up. Sliding in and out, faster and faster. Never in his life had anything been as good as being with Shayna.

Shayna gave a loud shout as her orgasm took her, then her head went back as she came, crying out his name, taking him with her, deeper than he'd thought possible as jet after jet of come filled her. He swore the world spun as he emptied himself inside the only woman he'd ever love. The only one he ever would. He'd said the Royce's didn't fall fast, but when they did it was forever.

He heard his voice echoing through the room even as they both quieted. He'd heard people talk about out of body experiences, but until that moment he'd thought they were full of shit. Hell, he still thought they were full of shit, but what he'd felt with Shayna went far deeper than just love. He'd give his life for the woman who lay over him. His dick twitched in agreement.

Shayna laughed. "Really, doesn't he know you need a recovery period?"

Mike lifted his injured arm and gave her a light tap. "Obviously he didn't get the memo."

They'd figure out what they were going to do about the future, but for now, he was happy right where he was and as long as Shayna was in his life, he'd be a happy man.

The End

Protecting Teagan

SEAL Team Phantom Book 6

http://www.elleboon.com/booklist/seal-team-phantom-series/

Dallas "Boomer" Holt ducked down as the MH-60 dropped him and the rest of their team off. Being the explosives expert on his SEAL team, he didn't care why they were in the middle of an ISIS stronghold, he just cared that they got in and got out. "Griffon, all is clear. We rendezvous with Grey and Rico at 0100."

The leader of his SEAL team studied the landscape below, it looked like nothing more than blackness with a few specks of light. Their intel had told them their target was being held somewhere in the middle of one of the buildings, but they wouldn't be able to drop in without being seen. They would make the rest of the trek in on foot, hopefully undetected with the cover of night.

"I don't understand why she wasn't with the other women in the first place. For fucksake, she was the richest one of the group. Hell, she'd have fetched a higher ransom than the three other ladies." Griffon looked through his night vision goggles, then turned back around.

Tyler "Griffon" Zarn was the leader of his SEAL team, and the oldest by a few years at thirty-four, followed by Gordon "Stroker" Jones who was coming up on his thirty-first birthday. Dallas shook his head as Stroker reached into his pocket, then flipped Griffon off.

"Yeah, that is what I give about why she wasn't with her friends. All I care about is getting the princess home and getting laid. You know how long it's been since I've gotten any from the female variety?" Stroker was their resident bad boy and considered two days without a woman too long. Of course, on a mission they sometimes had to go weeks without, but that was considered a hazard of the job.

"I'm assuming you haven't gotten laid by the male variety either, right?" Joey "Tamer" Hillman looked up from checking his weapons, his blond hair and blue eyes made him the all American good boy.

Again, Stroker stuck both hands in his pockets and came out with both middle fingers raised.

Joey shook his head. "I know I'm pretty, but I don't swing that way."

Griffon slapped Stroker on the shoulder while Dallas kept an eye on the trail in front of them. Ashton Lentz kept his on their back. Ashton, aka "Butler" was the quiet one of the bunch, but he could be counted on for just about anything, which was how he got his nickname.

"We got company coming, boys," Ashton spoke in a barely audible voice.

The five other members of the team had their weapons drawn and ready when Grey, Arcane and Zeb eased in like ghosts. Dallas didn't see the other three members of Grey's team, but knew from past experience, they would be coming in just as silently, and within seconds the three men arrived.

Griffon and Grey could be brothers in Dallas' mind. Both men had the same build and makeup, but it was the way they held themselves, which he assumed came from being in their positions.

"Rico's team is on the other side of the mountain. We'll split up and see if we can't find the target without incident. I have a feeling it's not going to be so cut and dried, or quite as easy as that, though," Grey glared down at the dark landscape.

Dallas wasn't sure what had put that look on his face and tone in his voice, but if Grey had a bad feeling, it didn't bode well.

"What do you know?" Griffon asked.

Grey stared around the group for a few minutes, then he sighed. "Nothing concrete, just the hair on the back of my neck is itching."

"Well fuck me running," Macon growled. His southern accent a little thicker than normal. He had all kinds of superstitions, and hair standing up was one of them as well. He was called "Snake", due to the fact he had a pet snake he called Conda and swore they were the best pets. The man also swore the thing could detect lies, but Dallas wasn't touching any of that with a ten foot pole.

Mitchem "Grey" Cappelli nodded. "Let's not waste time, boys." They all nodded.

"Eighteen heavily armed men are gonna be noticeable after a while even if we split up into groups of two." Snake had his KA-BAR knife in his hand as he spoke.

Mark pointed his thumb at Snake. "Is he certifiable?"

Griffon shrugged. "He passed the last psych eval."

It was Snake's turn to give the middle finger.

"Alright, let's head out. Boomer, you're with me. Tamer and Snake you two are together, and Stroker you go with Butler. Grey, I assume you'll split your guys up." At his nod, Griffon laid out the map. "We have a large area to cover. How do you want to do this?" He looked at Grey.

"Since Rico and his team have the North and East covered, we'll split the South and West up between us." Grey pointed out where each team would take up position.

"More than likely they'll have her in a building, and that building will be heavily guarded. Keep your eyes open for men who look suspicious. They should stick out like a stripper in Sunday school," Griffon said succinctly.

"What if there are a shitload of heavily armed men walking around?" Tamer asked seriously.

Grey put his hands on his hips. "Well then, we're fucked. Another thing that is gonna be a huge problem, is she'll blend in whether she's covered in the traditional clothing or not. With that in mind, we're looking for one woman who is more heavily guarded than any other."

"Whatever you do, remember, we are aid workers. Try to look not so…mean." Griffon looked at Snake and the knife he was using to clean his nails.

"Yeah, good luck with that," Zeb joked.

Griffon stilled. "Remember the main goal is to get in, get the girl, and get out without starting a war. We don't want to end up in the middle of that town down there shooting it up, killing god knows how many innocents. We all know that's the last thing either government wants. This is to be a snatch and grab assignment."

Dallas glared, knowing his nickname of Boomer was earned because he was not only the explosives expert, but because he tended to have a short fuse. However, he'd been doing a lot better, in his estimation. Of course, if the occasion called for it, he didn't mind blowing shit up. Like MacGyver, he could pretty much rig just about anything into a bomb.

After they all agreed on the course of action, they maneuvered down and made camp a little closer, then settled in for the night. "Get some rest men. If my gut's right, the next few days are gonna test us all." Grey and Griffon both ordered

Macon stabbed his KA-BAR into the dirt. "Y'all know she may not be fit to walk out of there, right?"

"This isn't our first rodeo." Grey stared around the team members. "If she can't walk, we'll carry her. If she refuses to come, we'll knock her ass out, and carry her. If she's scared shitless, you do what you can to reassure her, before knocking her out. Whatever we do, we do it fast, and we get the fuck out. Right, men?"

All eleven men nodded in agreement. Dallas had seen pictures of Teagan. The ones her family had been flashing on every news station. He was pretty sure if she hadn't been a high profile man's daughter, she wouldn't have been front and center of a SEAL rescue, but that didn't mean she didn't deserve to get out of the hellhole she was in. The entire world wanted the young woman home, but Dallas kept picturing the young yoga instructor smiling into the camera, telling everyone to get in tune with their inner selves, and wondered if she still thought that would bring her peace. Her world had been full of glitz and glamour, everything being handed to her on a silver platter. Now, she probably had things thrown to her on a dirt ground, or worse.

"We head out at first light. Get some rest. I have a feeling it might be our last for some time," Griffon said.

Dallas lay on his sleeping mat, lost in his musings of what the Hollywood Princess' life had been like since she'd been taken, compared to how it was before. Teagan Cross went in a vibrant young woman with her life full of promise on holiday with friends, facing something no woman should. What would she be like now after weeks in an ISIS stronghold?

****

Teagan woke with a start, her legs cramping from sitting with her knees against her chest. Every part of her itched, from her head to her filthy toes, but she preferred being dirty, to clean. If they allowed her to bathe, then they'd know what she looked like under her abaya.

The sound of murmurs reached her ears, but she didn't raise her head or make any move to let anyone know she was awake. Not speaking Arabic, she was at a total loss as to what anyone said anyhow.

She'd been in the same place for at least three weeks, maybe longer. Time was hard to keep track of while she'd been held captive. The large cinder block room they kept her and the other women and children in had windows too high for them to see out of, but allowed a little light in. However, there were bars over the windows, and the dirt was almost too thick, what sunlight did filter through wasn't a lot. At first she'd made marks in the dirt floor, but even that had been messed up in a shuffle of bodies. Now, she tried to keep track in her mind.

Hearing the unmistakable movement near the thick door, everyone tensed, knowing what it meant. She waited, holding her breath as a soldier stepped through, his gaze sweeping the area, searching for his next victim. Teagan kept her head on her knees, watching through her lashes. Since the first day she'd been taken, she'd learned the hard way not to look her captors in the eyes. These men…she used that term loosely, took a female looking at them in such a way as a direct insult or an invitation, resulting in a severe beating. She was still recovering from the fists of one soldier, and the pain of being hit from the butt of a gun from another, hitting her over and over. Teagan had no wish to experience the same brutality again.

Barely keeping from reaching up to touch her still sore ribs, she hoped her lack of movement kept her off the man's radar. Her sides ached from either being broken, or severely bruised. Either way, it hurt for her to take too deep of a breath. At first, she was sure a lung had been punctured, and worried she was going to die that first night, having coughed up blood. She'd cried happy tears, then cursed herself for the waste of precious fluids.

A spate of foreign language was issued, pulling her from her musings. A young man was jerked up and thrown out the door. Teagan winced as the woman who'd been next to him began to cry, making the soldier turn back and grab her too. The younger man looked to be begging the soldier, but was quickly subdued and both were hauled out, then the door was shut, the sound of a key locking them in again seemed overly loud. She wished she knew the language, having only herself to talk to, but feared speaking and letting those around her know she was an American.

She focused her mind, relaxed her legs until she was sitting cross-legged, going inside herself to escape her reality. Her Chakra was so out of whack, it took a while before she finally felt a calmness settle over her. Meditation was her only outlet, one that was short lived as hunger assailed, her stomach growling loudly. However, it was the only thing that had gotten her through the past few weeks, and she continued to breathe in steadily, then exhaling.

Wiping the sweat from her brow, glad she at least had enough moisture in her body to produce a little bit of bodily functions still. With her dark hair and dark complexion, she blended in better than her blonde friends had, but she didn't speak any foreign language except for a little Spanish. Now, she cursed her impulsive decision to go with her friends to another country on holiday. Hell, what did she know about other countries except they were foreign and she loved the food. She lived in California and owned a yoga studio for crying out loud. Her only saving grace had been her looks hadn't caused undue attention, so far.

Her mind drifted back to the day she'd been shopping with Lorie, Kally, and Carly.

"So, what do you think? Red carpet ready or what?" Teagan did a twirl, feeling the rough material swirl about her ankles. The black abaya and hijab combo instantly made her body temperature rise. The sundress below stuck to her like a second skin.

"Oh for sure. I mean, I can totally see Jessica Alba wearing it," Lorie Kline agreed.

The other two ladies rolled their eyes, but laughed good naturedly, walking away to look at other things. Teagan pulled the fabric away from her chest, already feeling sweat pooling between her breasts.

Before she could remove the garments, they were interrupted by shouts, and the sound of vehicle engines seeming out of place in the middle of the market. Teagan's eyes jerked up in surprise as several men piled out of trucks, barking orders in Arabic. Fear, the likes of which she'd never felt before, skated down her spine as she watched her friends being lifted into the back of the vehicle, weapons drawn on anyone who dared protest. She rushed forward, only to be knocked onto her ass, the end of a rifle smacking her on the side of her head. Stars danced in her vision, but she fought against the darkness trying to take her under.

Hard hands gripped her from behind, tossing her into another vehicle similar to the one that had taken her friends, only this one was filled with women dressed similar to her. It was then Teagan realized why she had not been put in the same vehicle along with her friends. Her captors thought she was a local, while her blonde, western dressed friends clearly were not. She opened her mouth to tell them who she was, but was faced with a gun pointed straight at her, its deadly intent clear. Lying in the street she saw her bag being picked up by one of the soldiers and tossed into the truck where her friends were, yet she couldn't see Lorie, Kally or Carly. Her head ached, and the feel of something wet dripped into her eyes. She swiped at it, seeing the smear of red on the tips of her fingers. All the fight went out of her as she collapsed onto the bottom of the truck bed surrounded by women and children of all ages.

The light began to fade when she opened her eyes again. Her stomach cramped from lack of any real food or water. If her captors meant to starve them all to death, then they were on their way to their goal. She couldn't remember the last time she'd had a meal, other than a couple bites of stale bread, and a sip of water, or liquid that was passed around as water every couple of days. A shudder rippled over her at the memory of the offending drink. However, in that moment, she'd gladly take a sip of it again. Her mouth was as dry as the air around her.

In the darkness, she chanced feeling her face with her fingers, glad she couldn't see the filth under her nailbeds. The feel of her cheekbones and other parts under the tips of her fingers felt normal, which was a good thing. Hell, she could look like the guy from the movie The Elephant Man, and wouldn't care if she made it home alive.

She woke as the door banged open, two men dressed in black robes stormed in, huge guns in their hands. They swept the area, looking for what she didn't know, but she held her breath, and prayed it wasn't her. God, she didn't know what she'd do if it was her. If they'd found out she was an American hiding amongst them, what would they do to her. She'd seen videos of what they did to their enemies. The beheading, and burning. Her stomach lurched. A sob threatened, but she forced it back. She was such a coward. Each time the door opened and they took another out, she knew they faced a horror the likes of which she didn't know, could only guess, and was glad it wasn't her. Now, she prayed it was someone else. What kind of person was she?

Teagan blinked, feeling no tears, which meant it had been way too long since she'd had any liquid.

Arabic words flew from one of the men. Heads of the other captors shook, so she followed suit. Then, they seemed to find who they wanted, a young girl. Again. Teagan bit her lip hard enough to make it bleed, and decided she couldn't watch another child go to his or her death. She was ready to die. Either from starvation, or by whatever means they chose. Whatever happened, at least she would have some input.

Her gut clenched as the soldier's eyes landed on the little girl Teagan had heard the mother call Adira. She couldn't be more than six or seven. Too young for whatever they did to them when they left their dirty cramped space. When it had been a woman, or young man, she'd closed her eyes and meditated, and although she'd hated to see anyone being taken, Teagan knew she couldn't protect them all, but this little girl was too young.

Before the man could jerk the child away from her mother's arms, Teagan jumped to her feet. "Stop, take me." Her voice cracked from lack of use and not enough water intake.

Her words had every head swiveling in her direction, and the soldier's gun coming up.

A spate of Arabic burst from him, then he rushed from the room, leaving her shaken. The young girl collapsed against her mother, who turned toward Teagan. "You are American?"

Teagan saw no reason not to answer honestly, and nodded, stunned to hear the broken English spill from the Middle Eastern woman's mouth.

"Thank you, but that was foolish," the woman said. "Now, you will be taken I fear. As will my child. You did a selfless thing for naught." Anger flashed in the woman's eyes.

The woman's almost perfect English shocked her. "What do you mean?" Teagan moved closer to the duo.

At closer inspection, she realized the woman speaking had green eyes, while her child had dark hair, brown eyes and dark coloring that matched the woman.

A sad look crossed her face. "I am Hanna. My husband thought we should visit his homeland. We were on holiday when he was...taken six months ago. We've been moved from place to place. I've waited for the day this would happen. Each time, I knew what I would have to do, or die trying." A shudder wracked her frail frame. "You should not have placed your safety in front of mine or my child's."

Teagan shook her head, taking in the resigned faces around her. "What's the difference if it's today or tomorrow, or next week? You and I both know it's going to happen, I just moved the timetable up some."

She so badly wanted to wake up and find the entire thing was a bad dream, but knew nothing would change her reality.

"What is your name?"

"Teagan Cross." Teagan stared at the door, knowing time was ticking.

As the woman got to her feet, two things slammed into Teagan's brain. The young mother was tiny compared to her, and two, she was very heavily pregnant. Like due any day. "Well, Teagan Cross, I'd say I owe you a debt, but fear I will never be able to repay you." Tears formed in the green eyes.

Her own eyes burned from the need to cry, because for the first time, she agreed, and hated it. At twenty-three, she hadn't lived yet. Sure, she owned a Jivamukti-Shakra Yoga Studio in Los Angeles that was thriving. But there was so much she had yet to do.

Teagan opened her mouth to reassure both mother and child, but the heavy door was thrown open, followed by several men entering with their guns raised. These men were also covered in the male version of the abaya, only they had weapons strapped to their waists and slung over their shoulders. Yeah, she knew her time had come. Not wanting them to come to her, she walked on shaky legs and took a few steps away from the pair cowering on the ground.

"Ah, the mute one has spoken I'm told. An American, too?" Hatred stared back at her from behind a red hijab, the masculine voice let her know he didn't need or want her to answer. His lips twisted in a cruel smile.

She stayed silent until one of the soldiers jerked her forward, grabbing the head covering from her and holding it in front of him like it was some sort of challenge. Words she didn't understand were yelled back and forth, and then the man with the red hijab backhanded the one holding her covering. Teagan knew her hair was a hot mess, yet she made no move to ease the heavy mass out of her face.

"Look at me, Ya Sharmouta." The soldier said in a hiss, making the others laugh. Teagan had no clue what he'd called her but assumed it wasn't a good name.

Doing as he'd said, she brought her eyes up to him, then wished she hadn't for he had the coldest, deadest eyes she'd ever seen. In them, she could see her own death, and all those around her. This man would take pleasure in the pain he caused.

He smiled, showing perfect white teeth in his swarthy face. "What is your name?" He held up his hand. "Before you think to lie to me, don't. I will find out and then you will suffer…more."

Hating herself, and this man for the fear he caused, she opened her mouth, then closed it as a cough caught her by surprise, bringing tears to her eyes. Her throat was drier than the desert she was in, and now, with the imminent threat of her own death, Teagan found she couldn't catch her breath.

He shook his head as if in disappointment, but she could see he was anticipating what was to come. "Bring her. We will clean her up a bit and see what she can do for us." He tossed her hijab back at her, and she hastily put it back on.

Chuckles from the men did nothing to soothe her. In fact, Teagan prayed she'd hack up a lung at any moment. Her prayers went unanswered as she was dragged in the leader's wake. The only good thing that came from her ordeal was that the young child was not taken with her, nor was her mother. In fact, nobody else was, except her.

About Elle Boon

Elle Boon is a USA Today Bestselling Author who lives in Middle-Merica as she likes to say…with her husband, her youngest child Goob while her oldest daughter Jazz set out on her own. Oh, and a black lab named Kally Kay who is not only her writing partner but thinks she's human. She'd never planned to be a writer, but when life threw her a curve, she swerved with it, since she's athletically challenged. She's known for saying "Bless Your Heart" and dropping lots of F-bombs, but she loves where this new journey has taken her.

She writes what she loves to read, and that's romance, whether it's about Navy SEALs, or paranormal beings, as long as there is a happily ever after. Her biggest hope is that after readers have read one of her stories, they fall in love with her characters as much as she did. She loves creating new worlds, and has more stories just waiting to be written. Elle believes in happily ever afters, and can guarantee you will always get one with her stories.

Connect with Elle online, she loves to hear from you:

www.elleboon.com

https://www.facebook.com/elle.boon

https://www.facebook.com/Elle-Boon-Author-1429718517289545/

https://twitter.com/ElleBoon1

https://www.facebook.com/groups/188924878146358/

https://www.facebook.com/groups/1405756769719931/

https://www.facebook.com/groups/wewroteyourbookboyfriends/

https://www.goodreads.com/author/show/8120085.Elle_Boon

https://www.bookbub.com/authors/elle-boon

https://www.instagram.com/elleboon/

http://www.elleboon.com/newsletter/

Other Books by Elle Boon

Ravens of War
Selena's Men
Two For Tamara
Jaklyn's Saviors
Kira's Warriors

Mystic Wolves
Accidentally Wolf & His Perfect Wolf (1 Volume)
Jett's Wild Wolf
Bronx's Wounded Wolf
A Fey's Wolf

SmokeJumpers
FireStarter
Berserker's Rage
A SmokeJumpers Christmas
Mind Bender, Coming Soon

Iron Wolves MC
Lyric's Accidental Mate
Xan's Feisty Mate
Kellen's Tempting Mate
Slater's Enchanted Mate
Dark Lovers
Bodhi's Synful Mate
Turo's Fated Mate
Arynn's Chosen Mate
Coti's Unclaimed Mate

Miami Nights
Miami Inferno

Rescuing Miami

Standalone
Wild and Dirty

SEAL Team Phantom Series
Delta Salvation
Delta Recon
Delta Rogue

Delta Redemption
Mission Saving Shayna
Protecting Teagan

The Dark Legacy Series
Dark Embrace

1-19

DISCARD

9 781725 636231